THE BAR
KILLER

A DR. GRAVES, M.E. THRILLER

H.L. ANDERSON

Immortal Works LLC
1505 Glenrose Drive
Salt Lake City, Utah 84104
Tel: (385) 202-0116

© 2022 Holli Anderson
https://www.holli-anderson.com/

Cover Art by Wilbert Stanton
wilbertstanton.com

This book is a work of fiction. Names, characters, businesses, organizations, places, events and incidents either are the product of the author's imagination or are used fictitiously. Any resemblance to actual persons, living or dead, events, or locales is entirely coincidental.

ISBN 978-1-953491-34-3 (Paperback)
ASIN B09T5X2ZZ1 (Kindle Edition)

To my brothers, Shawn and Troy (aka Pup) - the mean older brother who ended up being a big softy and the spoiled baby brother who would do anything for his family. I love you!

ONE

Carter's thumbs flew across the controller, and he leaned to the left as he made Mario jump over another stupid turtle. He loved it when he was the only one home because it was the perfect time to play his game without interruption. His dad was at work, and his mom, well, he didn't know, but she wasn't there, which meant his two-year-old brother wasn't there either.

Carter smiled thinking about Cody. It was kinda weird having a brother six years younger than him, but he was cool. He made Carter laugh a lot.

Something *thumped* upstairs and he froze.

His pulse sped up, heart pounding in his chest.

Another *thump* upstairs.

He pressed the pause button and turned the volume down—someone was in his parents' bedroom. Moving around, opening drawers.

Panic squeezed his lungs like a vise. Sweat broke out across his upper lip and dotted his brow.

A loud *bang* shook the house, and Carter curled up into a ball, covering his head. Something heavy crashed to the floor above.

His pulse thundered in his ears, almost too loud to focus on the noises upstairs. He rocked in place, waiting, his breathing rapid and unsteady.

He held his breath, still as a rock for several seconds, listening, but no other sounds came from the second floor.

Uncurling himself, he sat up, watching the stairs, his stomach tied in a tight knot. After a few moments, he rose to his feet, then shuffled to the stairs and looked up.

His breath seemed to echo in the silence, the only other sound was that of his heart pounding in his chest. He took the stairs slowly, one cautious step at a time. He hesitated on the last one, closed his eyes, then forced himself to lift his foot. He looked around the second-floor landing; all was quiet and darker than it was downstairs. He moved toward his mom and dad's bedroom, tried the doorknob. It turned easily, so he pushed the door inward, holding as still as he could.

His eyes landed on a pair of bare feet, toes pointing to the ceiling. He opened the door the rest of the way and stared at those feet. The thick toenails, calloused heels. His chest tightened with each breath, and his ears burned.

All moisture left his mouth, apparently finding his hands. He wiped his sweaty palms on his jeans.

I should call for help, he thought. But he wanted to see, so he stepped further into the room until his feet stopped moving, refusing to carry him any closer.

"Dad!"

He lay on his back. Blood and bits of gray goop were splattered across the carpet, with chunks of bone sprinkled among the mess.

Teeth.

Carter's stomach twisted uncomfortably, but a thrill of excitement skittered up his spine. He swallowed and licked his lips. His heart no longer merely pounded in his ears, but roared. "Dad..." But Carter knew he was gone. He didn't even have a face. Carter couldn't move his eyes from the sight before him. His chest seized, making it impossible for him to breathe. A weird thought floated into his mind, and the tightness of his chest relaxed as he inhaled at last.

Did it hurt when the bullet tore through your face, Dad?

And part of him hoped it did. He stepped closer. Closer still. Stopping only when he stood directly over the carnage, fascinated with the blood and brains and shattered teeth. The way Dad's face was just...gone. He bent and stuck his fingers inside the cavernous remains and smiled at the warmth of the blood and gore and the sucking noise his intrusion made as he dug even deeper.

TWO

PRESENT DAY
Dr. Graves

Dean Graves, Chief Medical Examiner of Augusta, was well known throughout the state as the M.E. who, through bad luck or God's sense of humor, ended up with the most bizarre cases of all the medical examiners in Georgia.

The detectives' laughter was annoying, though he should have been used to it by now. Why had he thought a medical degree specializing in forensic pathology would keep him from having to deal with living humans?

Dr. Graves shook his head, waiting for the detectives to gain control of themselves. He sighed. "Tracey, could you please control your detectives?"

"Enough!" Chief Billings snapped. "Report on the deceased." When Tracey Billings talked, people listened. Not a single officer in her precinct dared go up against her. Heck, not even the mayor—or the governor, for that matter—dared to cross the Chief of Police.

"Okay, okay. Sorry." Detective Troy "Pup" Fitzpatrick wiped his face. He gestured to the occupied body bag lying on the cold metal table. "This is a twenty-eight-year-old female—"

"A *human* female this time, I hope," Dr. Graves interrupted, half-mumbling as he unzipped the bag.

"Geez." Detective Shawn Davis grinned. "You bring a guy one dead skunk as a joke, and he never lets it go."

Dr. Graves looked up and scowled. "It took two weeks to get rid of that smell."

"Anyway…" the chief prodded.

Fitzpatrick wiped the smirk off his face and continued. "Like I said, twenty-eight-year-old female—*human*. Time of death fourteen-oh-five." He coughed, trying, unsuccessfully, to cover up another chuckle. "You finish, Davis. I need a drink." He barely made it through the motion activated doors before busting up again.

A steely gaze from Chief Billings put the serious back into Detective Davis. As a card-carrying member of MENSA—Dr. Graves was sure it was a fake—Davis was smart enough to know when to quit goofing off. He stood with his hands behind his back, in the "at-ease" pose of law enforcement officers. "At approximately thirteen-forty-five today, the deceased was riding with her husband in his overpriced sports car, probably speeding—"

The chief cleared her throat.

Davis glanced at her and continued, "She was in the passenger seat. They'd just left a Mexican restaurant ten minutes prior to the…incident."

Dr. Graves rolled his hand in a get-on-with-it gesture.

In a rushed jumble of words, Detective Davis blurted, "The deceased passed a large amount of gas, then she laughed, and her husband plugged his nose. The deceased said, 'You know you shouldn't feed me beans' right before she grabbed her chest and gasped. The husband thought she was joking around at first, but realized it was serious when his wife's lips turned blue. She lost consciousness as he pulled to the shoulder of the road. He called 9-1-1 and dragged the deceased out of the car to begin CPR. She was pronounced dead at the scene by the paramedics." Davis worked to keep his face neutral.

"Thank you," Dr. Graves said. "If I have further questions, I'll contact you."

Chief Billings nodded to the packet laying on top of the body bag. "The paramedic report is in there. I'll have Davis and Fitzpatrick email you their report as soon as they're done with it." She looked at Davis. "Let's go."

As they walked out the doors, Davis said, "Why is it that the only M.E. without a sense of humor always gets the hilarious cases?"

"There's nothing funny about death!" Dr. Graves yelled as the doors closed behind them. He shook his head and picked up the packet, walking as he read the report. He poked his head in his assistant's office. "Hey, Kat. Let's get started on the new arrival."

The day he'd hired Kat Flanagan had been one of his luckiest days. She knew how to take death seriously. Her curiosity and intelligence when it came to investigating the causes of death nearly matched his own.

Kat laid out the instruments while Dr. Graves finished unzipping the body bag. As soon as he saw the attire of the deceased woman, he had an idea—an unusual and unlikely idea—about what could have caused her early demise.

"Hand me the bandage scissors. These pants won't be easy to remove."

—∿—

As always, Dr. Graves dictated out loud as he performed the autopsy, the overhead microphone catching his oration. Kat had taken all the pre-autopsy radiographs and pictures and now stood across from him to assist. He sliced vertically down the abdomen. "No free blood was found upon opening the abdominal cavity in the midline. After gently moving the small bowel aside, it is noted that there are profuse air bubbles within the inferior vena cava." He slit open the chest and continued his dictation. "The chest was opened and the sternum was revealed superiorly with no disturbance of the vessels."

He stepped on the control that turned the dictation system off.

"Are you ready for the water, Dr. Graves?" Kat held a large syringe filled with clear liquid.

He nodded. "When I open the pericardial sac, fill it with water, gently."

"Can I ask why?"

Looking at her through the polycarbonate lens of a pair of safety goggles, he replied, "You'll see."

He clicked the recorder back on, and with great care, cut through both thin layers of the fibrous tissue surrounding the heart and great vessels. "The pericardial sac was opened anteriorly." He nodded to Kat and she injected the syringe-full of water into the sac. "Watch this," he said, a rare twinkle in his eyes.

As he cut into the vena cava now submerged in water, several large bubbles rippled to the surface, followed by a steady stream of smaller bubbles for a couple of seconds. He smiled up at his assistant, the only sign of which was the crinkling of his eyes, since his mouth was covered with a surgical mask.

"What the—" She stopped, looking up at the microphone dangling from the ceiling.

Dr. Graves continued his dictation, "An incision was made into the inferior vena cava below the line of water. A large volume of air was released as evidenced by several large bubbles, followed by approximately two seconds of a steady stream of smaller bubbles." He clicked the recorder off.

"So, Miss Flanagan, what do you think killed this woman?" He held the scalpel like a laser pointer, indicating the most recent incision.

She shook her head. "An air embolism, but...from what?"

"Very good." His eyes crinkled up in a smile again. "Let's finish this up, and then I'll tell you my conclusions."

THREE

Eighteen Years Ago
Carter, age 10

Cody, Carter's four-year-old brother, looked adorable in his little suit. Carter's smile turned to a scowl as he returned his gaze to his own reflection in the floor-length mirror. *Not me,* he thought. *I look ridiculous.* He pulled at the stiff collar buttoned all the way up to his neck.

His mom, nervous smile plastered to her pretty face, entered the room. "You boys look so handsome. We're almost ready to start. Cody, go stand with Mary now." She turned back to Carter and took his arm. "Are you ready to give away the bride?"

He tried, barely, to hide his resentment. He'd told her how he felt about Richard—Dick-wad, as he called him inside his head—several times. But she was "in love," whatever that meant. It had only been two years since his dad killed himself. A spasm of anger shot through Carter's chest. He ground his teeth and blinked back tears as he and his mom walked outside and waited for the stupid music to start. He glared at Richard, standing—no, *wobbling*—beneath the flowery arch at the end of the walkway between the rows of chairs. The man couldn't even stay sober long enough to get married. No, Richard would *never* be his dad. Never replace his dad. *I hate him.*

The music started and Carter and his mom began their slow march down the aisle.

Richard, eyes glossed over and half-lidded, tried to whistle as he leered at his bride, only managing to spray spittle across the first several rows of guests. He stumbled backward, catching himself clumsily by clamping his large hand around the pastor's arm, nearly pulling the man down with him.

Carter glanced at his mom. Her face was pulled into a rigid smile that looked more like a grimace, and her grip on his arm tightened painfully. Carter shook his head and growled under his breath, "Great choice, Mom."

The ceremony was a joke. And not a funny one. A cringy, what-the-hell-are-you-doing-Mom, stupid mess. His mom had to keep shaking Dick-wad's arm because he was falling asleep on his feet, swaying dangerously from side to side, front to back. He slurred his way through the vows, the pastor having to repeat them one word at a time for the idiot to say his part.

Little Cody, beaming up at their mom with a proud smile, presented the pillow with the cheap-ass rings tied to it to Richard. Instead of just taking the pillow from him, Dick-wad picked Cody up, babbling nonsense at the poor child. The drunk groom swayed, then stumbled a few steps backward as Cody let out a small scream. The best man pushed Dick-wad back into place before he could fall.

The look of terror on his little brother's face was more than Carter could stand. He flew from his seat in the front row and ripped the kid from the drunk's near-flaccid grip. He jerked his glare to his mom's tear-filled eyes. "Frick, Mom! Great choice. Really great frickin' choice."

—⋀—

A WEEK AFTER THE WEDDING, they all sat together at the kitchen table. Carter smiled as Cody waved his arms in excitement while he talked.

"...and the triceratops has three horns on its face! That's what I want for my birthday, Mommy, a triceratops!" The four-year-old spun around in his chair to look at his mom and bumped the small glass of milk next to his plate of mac and cheese.

Carter's smile faded as the glass tipped and the milk spilled onto the table. Dick-wad, too drunk to take evasive action, watched with his mouth hanging open as the liquid drizzled off the edge of the table and onto his lap in slow motion. The slug was able to find his speed then, as his hand shot out to smack Cody across the face.

Spit flew from Dick-wad's mouth as he shouted, "You stupid little bastard!"

Cody wailed, holding the side of his face as he struggled toward his mom. She glared at her new husband and yelled, "What is wrong with you? It's just a little milk!" She folded Cody into her arms, her tearful eyes shooting daggers at Dick-wad. "Don't you ever hit him again." Her voice shook and she diverted her gaze, looking down at the top of Cody's head.

"Yeah!" Carter glared at the freakin' drunk with narrowed, unwavering eyes. "Touch him again, and I'll kill you." His voice remained steady and strong as he held his spoon up like a shiv.

"Whatever." Dick-wad pushed his chair back and stood, steadying himself on the kitchen counter before reaching into the fridge for another beer.

FOUR

Present Day
Dr. Graves

"The category of death has been ruled natural, and the cause of death is an air embolus." Dr. Graves looked from Fitzpatrick to Davis, gauging their understanding based on the confused looks on their faces.

Fitzpatrick folded his arms and creased his brow. "Air...embolus? Explain."

"Yes, Dean." Chief Billings was the only one who called him by his first name. "Please continue."

Dr. Graves nodded. "The deceased's pants were real leather, unyielding and extremely...tight. So tight, I was unable to fit the trauma shears between them and her leg in order to get them off."

"So, death by tight pants?" Davis joked.

"That isn't what killed her, but it did play a big role," Dr. Graves continued, his face etched in solemn lines. "When the deceased passed a large amount of gas, as per the spouse's report, the gas had nowhere to go, as it couldn't permeate through the leather. Therefore, it took the path of least resistance—the vaginal canal."

Fitzpatrick snickered but stopped at a look from Chief Billings.

Narrowing his eyes at the detective, Dr. Graves resumed his oral report. "The gas, or air, from the flatulence traveled with some velocity into the deceased's vaginal canal, through a small laceration in the vaginal wall, and into her circulation, causing the air embolus found in the inferior vena cava that killed her."

Fitzpatrick and Davis looked at each other and let loose with the laughter they'd been holding in. Snorting, guffawing, disrespectful laughter.

"You two get out of here," Chief Billings ordered. "And get yourselves under control before you talk to the widower!"

"They have no respect for the dead." Dr. Graves shook his head, scowling after them.

"Dean." Billings put her hand on his shoulder. "Why is it that you get all the oddball cases?"

He shook his head. "I don't know. Statistically, the number of unusual death cases assigned to me is impossible. And I don't believe in luck—or unluckiness in this case." He shook his head again and pursed his lips. "I just don't know, Tracey."

"Well, I know one thing," Billings said, "I'm getting rid of my tight leather pants."

Dr. Graves cocked his head to the side and studied her for a moment. She hadn't cracked a smile when she'd said it. He had such a hard time picking up on sarcasm, but could not picture the stout woman standing before him as one who would own a pair of leather pants. He raised his eyebrows. "You...you own leather pants?"

Her straight face split into a smile. "No, just kiddin' with you. Can you imagine these thighs in a pair of tight leather pants?" She gestured to her lower extremities. "Yeah, me neither."

He breathed out and nodded. His assessment of Tracey had been correct after all. It really screwed up his day—or week, or month—when he evaluated someone's personality incorrectly. That didn't happen often, thankfully.

"Good work, doctor." Billings slapped him on the back. "I'm going to go lecture those two numbskull detectives of mine about proper decorum in the morgue." She walked toward the doors, then stopped and turned back to him. "By the way, what caused the vaginal laceration?"

Oh, good, a professional question he could easily answer. "It was consistent with a fingernail mark. Foreplay often consists of inserting the fingers into the vagina, and fingernails easily cut or abrade the friable tissue there. It isn't at all uncommon."

The chief nodded, her neck flushing pink as she turned back and walked out the doors.

FIVE

Present Day
Carter, age 28

Sitting in the bar for the third time in a week, Carter sipped a diet soda, cheering when the other patrons cheered, while pretending to watch whatever basketball game was on. His attention was really focused on one man sitting at the end of the bar. Williams was his name. He'd been there every night Carter had, like it was his first stop after work each night of the week. Carter crunched down on a pretzel and watched—trying not to glare—as the man downed another shot.

A loud, obnoxious ring tone blared from the drunk guy's pants pocket. His beer splashed on the counter when he slammed it down next to the empty shot glass and began the struggle to free the phone from his loose jeans. Carter watched as the man looked at the phone, squinting then scowling before jabbing a finger at the screen then holding it up to his ear.

"Whadya want, Sally? I'm busy," he slurred loudly.

The guy rolled his eyes and swayed on the stool. "I'll be home when I get home. Quit naggin' at me. And shut that kid up for hell's sake!" He ended the call. It took him several attempts to get it into his pocket again.

Carter waved down the bartender. "Give that guy another shot on me." He tipped his head in the drunk's direction.

"Okay," he said. "But this is the last one. I'm cutting him off and calling a cab after this one."

Carter nodded. Perfect. He paid his tab with cash, leaving a substantial tip, and left the bar.

He pulled his car to the curb at the front of the establishment and waited, excited pressure building in his chest. The drunk stumbled out the door and fell to one knee. Carter smiled and exited his running vehicle. "Mr. Williams?"

The dude was too far gone to answer. Carter stepped up to him and helped him to his feet before dragging him to the idling car. Carter mostly lifted him into the backseat and clicked the seatbelt around the now completely passed-out man.

$-\Lambda-$

THE FLOOR CREAKED in the old abandoned house as Carter stepped around to remove the tube from the man's throat. Carter smiled, almost laughing, at the crazed fear in his captive's eyes. As soon as the tube cleared the man's vocal cords, he screamed, long and loud, panting to catch his breath before starting again. Carter closed his eyes as the beautiful sound entered his ears and went straight to his soul like the music of a most exquisite symphony. The adrenaline surging through him proved too much, and he laughed and bobbed his head as he danced around the bound man, surveying his artistic handiwork.

The internal rush intensified as The Drunk fought his restraints now that the paralytic had worn off, begging, "Please. Please stop. No more. Please. It hurts. *Please!*"

The sound of terror in his voice, the pain apparent in his contorted face and bounding jugular vein, the copper smell of blood, the sick odor of feces and urine from where his bowels and bladder had let go with the first touch of Carter's scalpel—it all combined to overwhelm Carter with the need to do more. To inflict more pain. More damage.

His hands shook as he injected more of the magical paralytic drug into The Drunk's vein. They trembled as he forced the tube back into the man's trachea and pumped the bag. He'd never felt exhilaration like this. Never felt pleasure like this. This was definitely better than the first time.

Carter's heart raced with joy as he made the next incision, picturing Dick-wad—the abuser of his brother—as the one under the blade. This session would have The Drunk begging for death.

But Carter wouldn't rush, wouldn't give in to the man's pleas. He had all weekend.

He breathed in the magnificent scent of burnt flesh as he cauterized the incision, grinning as he whispered, "I wouldn't want you to bleed to death," near the man's ear.

This was the right thing. This would avenge Cody and their mom.

SIX

PRESENT DAY
Dr. Graves

A ringing phone at three in the morning was never a good thing. Doubly not a good thing for a Medical Examiner.

"Dr. Graves." He pressed the phone to his ear as he sat erect at the bedside.

"Hey, Graves, it's Fitzpatrick—"

"*Doctor* Graves, please."

Fitzpatrick sighed. "*Doctor* Graves. We have a murder scene we need you to come check out. It's...very unusual."

"It must be if you're waking me up in the middle of the night instead of just taking pictures of the scene." His voice held a bit of irritation. If he didn't get six-point-five to seven hours of sleep a night, he would be cranky for the rest of the day. And probably the next day. And maybe even the next, until his body returned to its normal rhythm.

"Sorry, doc. But we really need you to come take a look at this set-up."

Dr. Graves sighed. "Fine. Send me the address. I'll be there as soon as I can."

The site turned out to be a small abandoned house in the Laney Walker neighborhood. The CSI team had lights set up outside. Dr. Graves felt like he was traversing the red carpet as he stepped down the cracked and broken walkway toward the dilapidated porch. Slivers of light peeked out the boarded-up windows, and the door, once crisscrossed with two-by-fours, now stood ajar. He stopped on the porch, standing in what looked to be the sturdiest spot, the place that had the most boards still side-by-side. He slipped shoe covers over his loafers, then picked his way across the broken boards and into the house.

"Dr. Graves," a uniformed police officer said. "The detectives are waiting for you. Follow me."

He didn't need an escort. He could see the lights shining through a doorway not twelve steps away. Dr. Graves shook his head and followed anyway.

The photographer stood in the doorway, camera turned at an angle, trying to get a shot. When she moved to the side, Dr. Graves looked in the ramshackle kitchen. He would have gasped if it was in his nature, but it wasn't, so instead, his eyes just widened a fraction.

"Dr. Graves," Detective Fitzpatrick said. "Come on in. Tell us what you think of this."

"I'm no profiler," Dr. Graves said as he stepped closer, "but whoever did this has some serious issues." His gaze roved over the meticulous set up.

The victim lay on a table, with straps across his chest and legs. Dr. Graves stooped to look closer. They were tie-downs, like people used to secure a load or ATV, and they were cinched tight, cutting into the victim's skin.

"What do you make of this?" Davis gestured to the table next to the man's head.

"That's an ET tube..."

Fitzpatrick screwed up his face. "Like extraterrestrial?"

Dr. Graves leveled his gaze at the detective. "No. Like an endotracheal tube. At some point during this...process...the killer had this man on life support."

"And," a crime scene technician added, "the killer wanted us to know that." With gloved hands, she held up the victim's arm, IV catheter still intact and hooked to an empty bag of lactated ringers.

Dr. Graves pulled a pair of nitrile gloves on and stepped closer to examine the body. "Although these injuries are substantial and grotesque, none of them are severe enough to have killed this man—by themselves or cumulatively."

Pointing at the victim's damaged genitalia, he asked, "Did you get pictures of this already?"

The photographer nodded.

"Hmm." Dr. Graves examined the injuries, inspecting each wound.

"Ugh!" Fitzpatrick groaned. "That's just...so...wrong!"

Still examining the injury, Dr. Graves said matter-of-factly, "He was alive when this occurred. These incisions were made at different times. Some of them are partially healed. Whoever did this used a scalpel or something equally as sharp and precise."

Fitzpatrick turned away, shoving his mouth into the crook of his elbow and retching.

"What's the matter, Pup?" the technician asked. "Weak stomach?"

Dr. Graves' mouth twitched a little, but it was against his ethos to show any sort of levity when dealing with death, so he quickly extinguished it.

Most of the men in the room had either a leg crossed or an arm protecting their groin area. All of them had a look of horror plastered to their faces.

After inspecting the rest of the obvious injuries, Dr. Graves said, "Okay. Get him bagged up and over to the M.E. office. I'll go get set up." Some autopsies could wait until the next day or longer to begin. Not this one. Dr. Graves had some suspicions and needed to collect blood and tissue samples right away.

—√—

THE AUTOMATIC DOORS BRUSHED OPEN, and after a few quiet footsteps, the light in the small office next to Dr. Graves' clicked on.

"Kat?" Of course it was Kat; who else would it be at this hour?

She usually arrived before him to check the log, sort through the paperwork, and prepare things for any pending autopsies that day.

She came out and leaned on the door to his office. "You're here early. That's never a good sign." She flipped the light-switch, blinding him for a moment as his eyes adjusted. "Why are you sitting in the dark?"

"I've been up since three. I'm just trying to decrease some of the damage done to my circadian rhythm."

"Fair enough." She entered his office and sat in the chair across from his desk. "I'm assuming we have a new case?"

He nodded. "I already sent some blood and tissue samples over to the lab with STAT orders. The chemicals I'm looking for have very short half-lives, and I didn't want to risk them becoming untraceable."

"Murder victim or...?"

"Definitely a murder victim." He sighed and rolled his shoulders. "Let's get started. This one's going to take a lot of documentation. Bring a male body image and a photo log; there will be way too many photos to keep track of just by dictating."

Seven hours and over a hundred photos later, Dr. Graves finished sewing up the victim's chest. His normally mildly disheveled dark hair stuck up all over the place when he took off his head cover, mask, gown, and goggles. He washed and dried his hands, wiping them on his scrubs after, as was his habit.

"You look exhausted," Kat said as she took her turn at the sink.

Dr. Graves ran a hand through his hair. "I am."

"When was the last time you ate something?"

He tilted his head. "Umm. Dinner. Last night." His stomach growled as if to emphasize its pitiful emptiness.

"Let's go shower—" Kat laughed. "I mean, separately, of course."

"Of course." Why on earth would he think otherwise?

"Yes, well"—Kat cleared her throat—"then let me take you to an early dinner before you go home and work on your circadian rhythm some more."

He looked at her for a few seconds, then nodded. They'd never eaten together in the year and a half Kat had worked there. Each of them always brought their own lunch and sat at their own desks in their own offices to eat. "Sure, that'd be nice. I didn't even think about packing a lunch at three o'clock this morning." He smiled. It was nice of her to worry about him not eating all day.

Kat smiled back, and they both just stood there awkwardly until she shook her head like a small fly buzzed about it, blinked, and said, "Okay then. I'll...uh...meet you back out here in about thirty minutes." She didn't even wait for his answer, she just turned and headed for the women's locker room and showers.

—⋀—

It was more habit than helpful, but Dr. Graves ran a brush through his wet hair anyway. As soon as it dried it would be in disarray again. It was a battle he no longer fought; he refused to use hair products and didn't have time for frequent haircuts to keep the curls and cowlicks under control. He sighed and put the brush back in his bag. "Well, it worked for Harry Potter," he mumbled.

He stared down at his phone while he walked back into the morgue.

"All ready?" Kat asked.

"Yeah, I—" He looked up at her and tilted his head. Something was different. Several seconds passed before he realized what it was. "Your hair looks different."

Kat raised an eyebrow and smirked. "Yeah. I left it down."

"Right. I don't think I've ever seen it down." He shoved his phone into his pocket. "Where do you want to eat?"

Following him out the doors, she said, "I was thinking the little diner just down the street?"

Dr. Graves nodded and headed for the elevator.

They walked to the diner in silence, Dr. Graves slowing his steps to make up for Kat's much shorter legs. He looked down at her. *I wonder how tall she is?* It wasn't something he'd ever considered before and wondered why he was considering it now. He'd been six-foot-two since the tenth grade; she stood about a foot shorter than him—below average height for a woman.

He reached the door to the diner first so he held it open for her. "How tall are you?" he asked as she stepped past him.

"Five-one and a half, why?"

He nodded. "About what I figured. Just curious."

"And how tall are you?" she asked with a quirk of her mouth.

He guessed turn-about was fair play. "Six-two."

She winked. Which was weird. She'd never done that back at the morgue. "About what I figured," she said before turning to tell the greeter, "Table for two, please."

They sat across from each other at a booth and ordered drinks—Kat a Diet Coke and Dr. Graves a water, no ice. He'd read studies that said ice was bad for your liver.

Dr. Graves only considered a handful of foods to be edible to his palate, so making a decision was not a long, drawn-out process for him. He set the menu down, expecting Kat to take considerably longer to make her choice. She looked up at him with another odd smirk, already having laid her menu on the table.

Stacking the two menus neatly together, he smiled. It seemed that he and his assistant were compatible in more ways than just work ethic.

The brawny male server brought their drinks. "Are you ready to order?"

"Yes, I believe so," Dr. Graves said. "I'll have a Caesar salad with grilled chicken."

"And you, ma'am?" His lips parted in a smile.

"I'll have a grilled cheese sandwich and fries." Kat pushed a strand of brunette hair behind her ear.

The server gathered up the menus. "I'll have that right out."

Dr. Graves had never been good at small talk, so he just didn't participate in it. They sat in silence until Kat leaned forward and folded her arms on the table. "So, Dr. Graves, what do you do for fun?"

He cleared his throat, then said something he'd never said to anyone before—at least not since graduating from medical school. "I think we've worked together long enough that you can call me Dean...outside of work, of course."

"Okay," she said, a slight hesitation in her tone. "Dean, what do you do for fun outside of work?"

Did it feel as weird to her as it sounded to him for her to call him by his given name? "I...umm... I paint."

"Oh? What kind of paint? Oils, watercolor, acrylic, house?" Kat smiled.

"Oil, mostly. I dabble a little in watercolor."

"What kind of subjects do you like to paint?"

"I..." Oddly, he hesitated to tell her that he mostly painted flowers. And he suddenly decided that maybe participating in small talk wasn't such a bad thing. "What do *you* like to do for fun?"

Kat narrowed her eyes at him for a brief second. "I like to read."

"Fiction or non-fiction?"

"Fiction. I got my fill of non-fiction in college. Do you read anything besides medical books?" she asked.

Dr. Graves raised his eyebrows. "Of course I do. One can learn a great deal from fiction. Not to mention that sometimes leaving this world for a bit is necessary—especially in our line of work."

She opened her mouth as if to speak then closed it and shook her head. "I didn't expect that from you."

He tilted his head to the side. "Why not?"

"Well, you just seem..." She looked up at the ceiling, obviously searching for the right words. "You're so serious all the time. I just figured you for a non-fiction guy." She shrugged.

"Serious or boring?" He cracked half a smile.

"Oh no!" Kat said. "Not boring at all. I find you fascinating!" Her face turned slightly pink, and she suddenly found her silverware to be mesmerizing.

Of course she found him fascinating; he *was* fascinating. Why was that embarrassing for her?

Women are so unpredictable.

The server brought their food and laid the plates in front of each of them, warning Kat, "Your plate is hot; be careful." He slid a small slip of paper across the table to her. "Not as hot as you, though." He winked and walked away.

Dr. Graves took a bite of his salad, eyeing the slip of paper. "What did he give you?"

Kat rolled her eyes. "I think you can figure it out." She stared at her plate, her skin flushing a darker shade.

"It's too small to be the bill..." he mused. "Is it a coupon?"

Her eyes finally met his and widened. "You're serious." It wasn't a question or a sarcastic remark. "It's his phone number, Dean. He gave me his phone number."

He set his fork across his salad bowl. "Why? Do you know him?"

Kat laughed and her face returned to its normal color. "No, Dr. Graves, he gave it to me because he thinks I'm 'hot'."

"Oh." He picked up his fork again, then jerked his head up to look at her. "*Oh.* He wants to *date* you. I've never been good at picking up on the cues of human attraction." He stabbed a slice of chicken harder than was quite necessary. Why did he feel annoyed? It must just be from lack of sleep.

"No kidding," Kat mumbled before taking a large bite of her sandwich.

He watched her chew as she stared out the window. She *was* attractive. Her eyelashes curled in a perfect arc, reaching just below her brow. Her eyes, he noticed for the first time, were the color of chocolate orchids—one of his favorite flowers to paint. Her skin, unblemished and smooth...

Turning back to her sandwich, she caught him staring at her. "What?" she asked. "Do I have something on my face?" She wiped her mouth with her napkin.

Dr. Graves cleared his throat and concentrated on his salad. "No. I was just..." He shoved a large bite into his mouth.

The conversation for the rest of the meal centered around work and their latest case.

The phone-number-giving server rushed to help them at the cash register, nearly bowling over a female coworker. He took the check from Kat and grinned. "Not much of a gentleman, making the lady pay."

"I asked him to dinner," she hurried to explain.

"Well..." He leaned in and fake whispered, "If you asked me out, I'd insist on paying."

Kat laughed and handed him her credit card.

A strange feeling welled up in Dr. Graves' gut, along with a strong urge to throat punch the guy. *Is this what jealousy feels like? Or am I coming down with something?* He shook his head. "I'm going to head home now, Kat. Thank you for dinner. I'll see you tomorrow morning."

SEVEN

The knife glinted from the light of the television as Carter gripped the handle with both hands, the point of the blade hovering over his stepdad's chest as he lay on the couch in a drunken stupor, mumbling incoherently. The boy's hands shook, and his rage-filled heart pounded against his ribs. *Just do it! Quit being a chicken!* But the resolve he'd had a few minutes ago when standing in the kitchen over the knife drawer was waning. He couldn't do it. He dropped his head, lowered his arms, and gave one last disgusted look at Dick-wad before trudging back into the kitchen to return the knife to its drawer.

—∿—

Carter kicked a rock down the road as he ambled home from school, in no hurry to get there. For the first time in his life he wished he played sports so he would have an excuse to stay late after class. He gave the rock one last hard kick, blasting it into the neighbor's fence before heading into his own yard with a heavy sigh.

"How many *effing* times do I have to tell you!" Dick-wad's booming, slurring voice broke through Carter's sulk.

Carter ran the rest of the way to the front door and barreled inside, stopping to take in the scene before him.

Dick-wad gripped Cody around the neck with both hands, lifting his feet inches off the floor. With a roar, Carter launched himself at his much larger stepdad. Dick-wad jerked his head in Carter's direction, dropped Cody, and body-checked the older boy into the wall.

Carter crumpled to the floor with a moan, dazed.

The drunken man pointed at him. "Stay out of this!" He lumbered back to the cowering six-year-old and grabbed the front of his shirt, twisting his fist in the cloth. He lifted the boy to his feet, then back-handed him across the face with a loud *smack*.

"I warned you, you little git!" Spittle flew in Cody's face as Dick-wad yelled. He pointed to Cody's backpack leaning against the wall by the front door. "That's not where that goes." The boy's head lurched back and forth as the man shook him, spraying blood from his split lip onto the man's filthy t-shirt, the carpet, and the worn couch. "Now *go put it away!*"

Carter followed his sobbing little brother to his room, where they stayed until their mom came home from work. Dick-wad lay passed out on the couch. Cody ran to his mom and, with one look at his face, she dropped to her knees, pulling him to her chest. She rocked back and forth, sobbing, kissing his head, and muttering, "I'm sorry, Code. I'm so sorry. He doesn't mean it. It's the booze."

"Mom!" Carter whisper-yelled. "Listen! He isn't going to stop! This is like the sixth time!" He bent down, closer to her splotchy cheeks, and hissed, "You need to kick him out."

She shook her head, still rocking and sobbing.

Carter rubbed his arm where it had slammed into the wall and screwed up his face in anger. "You're a coward," he breathed, just inches from his mom's face. He clamped his jaw so tight he thought his teeth might crack as he stood and stalked off to the kitchen to make an ice-pack for his little brother.

I'm a coward too. I should have plunged that knife into him when I had the chance. I hate myself.

EIGHT

PRESENT DAY
Dr. Graves

The two weeks following their impromptu dinner, Kat had kept her hair up in the usual ponytail and conversations had been focused only on work-related subjects, though he'd caught himself multiple times on the verge of asking her what she'd done with that server's phone number. And, he had painted an unusual number of paintings involving chocolate orchids...

"We have your results, Dr. Graves. I'll send those right over." The exasperated voice on the phone brought him back to the issue at hand.

"Two weeks"—Dr. Graves worked not to raise his voice—"is that what STAT means to your lab?"

"Yes, two weeks *is* STAT. Blood and tissue analyses usually take four to six weeks."

"I know. And I still think it's a ridiculously long time. Thank you for your assistance." He hung up the phone and yelled for Kat. There was no sense in using the phone to call her since their offices were only steps away from each other.

She appeared in his doorway a split second later. "Yeah?"

"Call Chief Billings and tell her the Williams report will be ready in thirty minutes." He refreshed his email for the third time since getting off the phone twenty seconds ago.

"Okay."

Finally, the encrypted email from the lab popped up. Dr. Graves typed in his password and printed out the lab results. He just needed to add this to his report, finish writing his conclusion with this new evidence, and print out two copies, one for the police and one for his own files.

Kat appeared in his doorway. "She said she and the detectives will be here in an hour for a face-to-face briefing. She sounded worried."

"She should be. I'm afraid a killer like this isn't going to stop at one."

—∿—

THERE WAS no childish snickering or off-color remarks from Detectives Fitzpatrick and Davis today. Dr. Graves imagined they were still seeing the damage done to this man's body in their nightmares.

Chief Billings stood with her arms crossed over her ample chest, worry lines creasing her face. She nodded to Dr. Graves. "You get these reports back faster than any other M.E. It would have been at least another three weeks for anyone else."

"You know I hate having a backlog. Plus, the families deserve better." He studied the papers in his hands and began his oral report as he always did. "The category of death has been ruled murder. The cause of death: asphyxiation."

"Wait," Davis said, "you mean none of those...injuries caused his death?"

"No, they did not." Dr. Graves looked down at the report in his hands and suppressed a shiver. "The victim was alive for each and every one of the injuries present on his body." He looked up, and his grip tightened around the paper, crinkling it. "And, he was awake and aware for all of them."

"But...how?" Chief Billings asked. "The injuries were so...precise, and the restraints we saw would not have been nearly enough to keep him still while..."

"No," Dr. Graves agreed. "They wouldn't have."

"What about the ET tube thing?" asked Fitzpatrick. "What was that all about if not to knock the guy out?"

"I'm getting to that."

"Why don't we let Dr. Graves finish giving the report, and then ask questions," Kat suggested.

The three officers nodded and looked toward the doctor.

"Thank you." Dr. Graves dipped his head at his assistant. "I will give you the facts first, followed by my scientifically-based assessment of what likely happened. During the five days the thirty-eight-year-old male victim was presumably held captive, he suffered one-hundred-twenty-five external injuries—"

Detective Davis sucked air in through his teeth, shaking his head.

"—including: seventy-two lacerations, twelve fractured bones, degloving of two fingers, amputation of two toes, crush injuries to three fingers and three toes, had four teeth knocked out in a violent manner, both tympanic membranes pierced, both eyeballs punctured, twenty-three distinct and separate hematomas, and his tongue removed." Dr. Graves pulled in a breath. "Each of these injuries appear to have been inflicted at different times throughout the five-day period as evidenced by the differing healing patterns. For a complete surveillance of these injuries, please see the body diagrams included in the report."

Dr. Graves rolled his shoulders, trying to stave off the aches he was sure to have later from holding them so tense. "Internal injuries consisted of a lacerated kidney, a punctured small bowel, three lung contusions, and abrasions and small tears to the vocal cords and trachea from repeated intubations."

The detectives both shuffled their feet, and Fitzpatrick wrapped his hand around his throat protectively.

Dr. Graves' eyes flicked up to them briefly as he continued, "Incidental findings unrelated to the injuries were: diffuse steatosis of the liver with early signs of cirrhosis, gastritis, and microscopic varices in the esophagus. These findings indicate the victim was a heavy drinker."

He made eye contact with Chief Billings. "And the lab results—this is where your investigation will likely narrow. The victim's plasma came back positive for choline, indicating that the victim was dosed with the paralytic, succinylcholine."

Chief Billings shook her head. "What's that? Some new club drug we haven't heard of yet?"

"No, nothing of the sort." Dr. Graves leaned forward. "It's a paralytic, meaning it paralyzes the entire body, including the ability to breathe. It's used every day for surgeries and emergent intubations, but always with the addition of a strong sedative that puts the patient into an unconscious state. Otherwise," he ran a hand through his hair, "the patient would be aware of and feel every bit of the surgery, unable to move even their eyes to alert the medical staff of their excruciating pain."

Kat had already heard this, but still she covered her mouth and squeezed her eyes shut at hearing it again.

"So..." Davis gulped. "He, the victim, he *was* awake for all of"—he waved his hand over the report he held—"this?"

Dr. Graves nodded.

"I think I need to sit down," Davis said.

"Yeah, me too, partner," Fitzpatrick agreed.

"Let's go to my office," Dr. Graves suggested. "Kat, could you please grab a couple of folding chairs?"

Once everyone was settled in the doctor's small office, Chief Billings asked, "What do you think, Dean? What the hell happened to this poor man?"

"My theory is that the perpetrator coerced him from the bar where he was last seen and likely highly inebriated, and brought him to the house where he was found. The perp started an IV and strapped the victim to the table." Dr. Graves stopped, his eyes glazing over for a moment as he imagined the scene, the terror. He shook his head and cleared his throat, beginning again in a quieter voice. "When the victim was completely awake and aware of his surroundings, the perp injected the succinylcholine and intubated the victim. This is where it becomes a little tricky; I picture one of three scenarios here." He raised his right hand to count down on his fingers. "One, the perp acted alone and used an Ambu bag to administer breaths to the victim while he was paralyzed. This would mean that he would have to pump the bag to give a breath, inflict his torture but not take more than about twenty seconds, then pump the bag again, repeating until he was...finished, thus working alone.

"Two, he had an accomplice who worked the bag for him—I find this scenario highly unlikely."

Chief Billings, leg bouncing up and down like a piston, nodded. "Yeah, I have trouble imagining *one* person that's sadistic enough to do something like this, let alone two."

"Exactly," Dr. Graves agreed. "The third possible scenario is that the perp has access to a portable respirator, though this is also unlikely."

He tapped his fingers on his desk and avoided eye contact with the others. "I think the perp allowed the paralytic to wear off between torture sessions, thus the need for the restraints. Plus, a psychopath like this, I would think, would want to taunt his victim and see the reaction. When he was satisfied with his work—or because of some other time constraint—after five days, he dosed the victim with the succs again and let him die of asphyxiation, unable to breathe on his own."

He laid the report on his desk and looked around the room, met by utter silence.

Kat, surprisingly, was the one to break the silence. "Where would he have gotten the succinylcholine?"

"Yeah," Fitzpatrick said, "that doesn't sound like something you could get out on the streets."

Dr. Graves nodded. "It isn't. This is where your search for the suspect narrows. This person works in a hospital or surgical center.

The only places that use paralytics are ORs, ERs, and ICUs—the last two when they need to intubate someone."

"So, are we looking at a doctor, here?" asked the chief.

"Maybe. The suspect would have to have full access to the medication, and that's more likely in an OR. If I had to make an educated guess, I'd say it's an anesthesiologist or a nurse anesthetist because they would have the greatest opportunity to divert the amount of drug needed for this...crime."

"Don't hospitals keep track of this stuff?" Davis' voice rose at the end.

"Yes. So that brings up another theory. Independently owned surgical centers are more lax on the rules—some of them anyway—than hospitals are. So you should start there."

"My assumption would be," the chief said, "that he wouldn't be getting this drug from just one place. It would be too easy to be caught stealing it." She looked at Dr. Graves. "Would it be unusual for this type of doctor or nurse to work at several different facilities?"

"Good question. And the answer is no. Many surgical centers hire anesthesia providers on an as-needed basis, leaving time in their schedules to work at multiple different places."

"Chief," Fitzpatrick said, "you've both been saying 'he.' I know that most murders are committed by men, but this one just seems so... I don't know...*personal*. Are we even going to consider that this might be a scorned woman?"

She narrowed her eyes at the detective. "I'm gonna let the doc answer this one."

"The chances of this being a female are infinitesimal, detective." Dr. Graves folded his hands together on his desk. "Men tend to be the ones who torture when they kill, women are more likely to poison their victims. The victim was a big guy, and if my guess about him being extremely inebriated is correct, he would have needed a great amount of assistance to and from a vehicle and into the house. Then there are issues of testosterone and rage..."

"But, don't guys like this usually kill chicks?" Davis asked.

"By 'chicks' I assume you mean women?" Dr. Graves' jaw muscle twitched. "The answer is yes, and that's a good point. But I still think we're looking at a male killer here."

"Okay, boys." Chief Billings stood and slapped the detectives on their shoulders. "We start with the surgical centers. Get a list of all surgical centers within a fifty-mile radius of that bar where Mr. Williams was last seen."

The detectives left the office and Chief Billings turned back to Dr. Graves. "Thank you for your insight on this case. I'll keep you apprised of the investigation. I have a feeling I'm going to need to pick your brain some more."

"Of course. Whatever you need, Tracey." When she left the office, Dr. Graves put his head in his hands and rubbed his temples with his thumbs.

"Getting a headache?" Kat asked.

He nodded.

"I'll get you some acetaminophen."

—⌇—

THE RAIN POURED DOWN, making little splashes in his pond as Dr. Graves stared out at the forest bordering his property. He loved the spring rains in Georgia and often sat on his covered porch to experience them. He breathed in deeply; the smell of fresh rain never got old. He lifted the bottle of home-brewed cream soda to his lips; it was the only thing he drank besides water.

As hard as he tried to separate work from home, his thoughts kept drifting to the killer. What kind of person would do this? What was his motivation? And the worst thought of all:

He's going to do this again.

Dr. Graves set aside the book he'd been trying to read and picked up his phone. He had a strange desire to call Kat and talk it over with her. Maybe that would help clear his mind so he could go to sleep at a decent hour.

She picked up on the second ring. "Hey, boss. What's up?"

"Just sitting on the porch, watching the rain."

"O-*kay*. Did you need something?"

He shouldn't have called. It was Friday night; she probably had plans. What if she was on a date? A wave of discomfort crashed into the walls of his stomach, and he rubbed his hand there, wondering again if he was coming down with something. "Sorry. It can wait if you're busy."

She laughed sardonically. "Unfortunately, I am rarely busy on a Friday night. Are you okay?"

Dr. Graves' jaw relaxed. "I'm fine. I just can't stop thinking about the killer. I thought that maybe if I talked it over with someone, I'd be able to get it off my mind for a while—at least long enough to sleep."

"Oh, sure." Her voice went from fake-forlorn to...interested? Pleased? "Do you want me to come over? Or...or meet you somewhere?"

His intention had been to just talk on the phone, but maybe talking in person would be better. Talking on the phone was not something he enjoyed. "Okay. Yes. Where would you like to meet?" It would be inappropriate to invite her to his house.

"How about the brewery over by the river?"

"You know I don't drink alcohol..."

He could almost hear her eyes rolling in her voice. "I know you don't, but I do. And they serve water. They'll probably even serve it to you without ice if you ask nicely."

This outside-of-work version of Kat was a little snarky. He kind of liked it. A small grin tugged at his mouth. "Meet you there in ten minutes."

"Make it twenty. I live a little farther from it than you do." She ended the call without even saying goodbye.

—∿—

It was early enough in the evening that the place wasn't packed yet. Kat arrived just after him, her hair down around her face again. They were seated at a booth, away from the noise of the bar. Kat ordered a beer with some weird name and something called "mac and cheese poppers."

Dr. Graves ordered water without ice.

"Separate checks?" the waitress asked with a smile.

"No, I'm buying tonight," Dr. Graves answered.

"Oh…" The waitress's smile disappeared. "I was sort of joking, since water is free and all."

"Right." He nodded. "Even so, I'll be paying."

The waitress took their order to the back.

Kat laughed. "I think you disappointed her in a couple of ways. And you don't need to pay for my order."

"What do you mean I disappointed her? And you bought last time so it's my turn."

She shook her head, a quirky smile turning her lips into a work of art, the color of apple blossoms. "For such a smart man, you can be utterly clueless sometimes."

"I've heard that before," he mumbled.

"Well"—she folded her arms on the table—"in this instance, the waitress was flirting with you and you didn't reciprocate. Also, you didn't get her joke. And lastly, she was hoping I was going to pay for my own order."

"Flirting? How can you tell? And why would she care who pays?"

"How to explain signs of flirting to an intellectual introvert…" Kat reached across the table and brushed her fingers across his hand. "She touched you when she introduced herself—number one sign a woman is flirting with you. She barely looked at me and couldn't take her eyes off of you. Her tone of voice changed when she was talking to you, a little higher pitched with some added sugar. She cared about who was paying because she was hoping this isn't a date." She added quickly, "Which it isn't, of course. But you paying makes it appear as if it is."

His hand still felt warm from where Kat had touched it. The waitress's touch hadn't felt at all like that. Maybe Kat was coming down with something... He shook his head. "I don't think I'll ever understand women."

"Probably not," Kat agreed.

"Thanks for having so much confidence in my ability to learn." He smiled. "It's weird, I notice the smallest of details when performing an autopsy or going over a crime scene, but I've never been able to tell when someone is flirting with me."

"I've noticed that."

He cocked an eyebrow. "When have you noticed? This would have been your first opportunity to..." The brief look of panic that raced across her face stopped him short. Had *she* flirted with him? He searched his memory for any of the signs she'd just told him about. Not at work; Kat was too professional for that. Wasn't she? He rubbed the top of his hand where she'd touched him just a moment ago. Her hand did sometimes brush against his when she handed him something—but that was just accidental, right?

He glanced up, and her face had turned a shade darker than a Crimson Glory rose. She stared down at her hands.

Dr. Graves cleared his throat. "I may never be able to discern when someone is flirting with me. I'm a hopeless cause." His heart skipped a beat. Weird. Palpitations weren't all that abnormal, but he hadn't felt one before. "Perhaps women who are interested in me will need to take a more direct approach."

A wry smile touched Kat's lips. "Duly noted."

The waitress brought their drinks and smiled at Dr. Graves. "The appetizer will be out shortly."

"Great," he said. "Thank you."

She walked away. *Now would be a good time to change the subject.* He glanced at Kat, whose skin color had returned to mostly normal. "So, this murderer. The police need to find him quickly, before he does this again. My thoughts keep swirling around and around like a flushing toilet, so I thought if we talked it out, maybe we could find some way of helping the detectives figure this out."

"Okay." Kat nodded. "Tell me what you've been thinking about."

"Well, first, this was obviously someone filled with rage, so it has to be personal. Not necessarily that he knew the victim or had a vendetta against him—but someone the victim reminded him of."

"That is how most *serial* killers work," Kat agreed, "but this was just one murder."

"Yes, well, all serial killers have to start somewhere." He tapped on the table with his fingers. "I don't know about you, but I don't want to do another autopsy like that ever again."

"Agreed." She pushed her hair behind her ears. "But we need to look at all angles if we're going to be of any help. What if the victim was sleeping with the killer's wife? Or hurt someone the killer loved? I mean, obviously, what he did was complete overkill, but..."

Dr. Graves shook his head. "I can't see it being that. Murders that come from things like that are crimes of passion—unplanned, quick, sloppy. This was none of those things. This was meticulously planned. It would have taken weeks for the killer to amass enough succs for what he did."

"And it was so demented," Kat added. "Only a psychopath of the highest degree would think to do something like this."

"Yes, exactly. And that goes back to my original train of thought: he chose that abandoned house for a reason. That meant something to him. And the victim, well, my guess is that he didn't know the victim, but that the victim was a 'type.' He reminded the killer of someone."

"So, maybe the police should find out some history on that house," Kat said. "They could crosscheck it against what they find at the surgical centers—see if any names are associated with both."

"Great idea. I'll talk to Tracey about it on Monday." He reached across the table and touched her arm. It was an act of spontaneity so very unlike him, he almost jerked his hand back. Instead, he left it there for far too long as he said, "This is really helping, thank you for agreeing to talk with me." He slid his hand back to his side of the table and sat back.

The waitress sidled up and set Kat's order down between them. She refilled Dr. Graves' water. "Can I get you anything else?"

"No," Kat answered. "I think we're fine now."

Her smile faltered. "Alrighty then. I'll be back in a bit with the check."

After she was far enough to be out of hearing range, Kat smiled at Dr. Graves. "You're welcome. What other thoughts have been keeping you awake at night?" She blew on one of the deep-fried, battered, macaroni and cheese filled arterial plaque-makers, then popped it in her mouth.

Dr. Graves watched her chew a few times before answering. "Well, the killer has to be old enough to have graduated from college and some sort of graduate program if my thoughts of him being a doctor or advanced-practice nurse are correct. Yet, as far as we know, this is his first act of such violence. I did a search for similar murders, and nothing popped up." Kat nodded, so he continued, "I'm just going to run this scenario by you. This man had something terrible happen to him when he was young. Or several terrible things, at the hands of someone close to him. A teacher. A religious leader. A scout leader. His own father or other family member. He repressed it. He had to have in order to become a nurse or doctor, that takes years of deliberate focus. Then, recently, something happened to set him off. Something that reminded him of the terrible thing or things he suffered as a child or teen, and it broke something loose in him. Something dark. A mental illness that had been lurking there.

"So he chose a victim that reminded him of the person that hurt him—"

"Could the victim have been the person that hurt him?"

"Could have been." Dr. Graves took a sip of water. "But I don't think he was. Some serial killers start by murdering the person who they perceive as having harmed them, but that murder is typically unlike the others. And it's hidden. It's too personal to share with the world. He wanted this victim to be found. He wanted to show off his work."

"How was he found?" Kat asked.

"Tracey said the killer had pulled his car into the backyard where it couldn't be seen by the few people still living in that neighborhood. He'd used the back door as an entrance when he and the victim arrived. But, sometime before leaving the house and the body behind, he pulled the boards off the front door and opened it, leaving it open for a passerby to see."

"I assume the police are following up on any tire prints left in back of the house?" Kat asked.

"Yes. That analysis has already been done. They come from a very common tire, unfortunately, sold at almost every tire store around."

"Is there anything in this line of thinking that can help the police?" she asked.

"I don't know. Maybe. Maybe they should dig a little deeper into any other unsolved murders that have been committed recently, within the past six months maybe, see if there's any connection." He shook his head. "I just don't know."

"I think that's a good idea. Maybe we can help. I know the police are busy. Maybe you can offer to go through those files and I can help you."

That thought sent a flush of warmth through his chest. Not the thought of looking through murder files, but the thought of Kat helping him. "I'll do that. I'll ask Tracey to have someone pull the files from Augusta and surrounding counties—maybe all of Georgia."

Kat raised an eyebrow. "Let's start with a few counties first."

The flirty waitress walked up to the table and handed the check to Dr. Graves. "I'll be your cashier." She leaned in and whispered with a wink, "And anything else you want me to be."

Dr. Graves' gaze flicked to Kat, whose mouth was agape as she watched the waitress walk away, then he slipped cash into the folder and set it on the table. Shaking his head, he said out loud to himself, "What on earth would make her say that?"

He hadn't expected an answer, but Kat gave him one anyway. "You seriously don't know? You are a very handsome man, Dean. Do you even own a mirror?"

NINE

Sixteen Years Ago
Carter, age 12

Carter sat in the swing, holding to the rusting chains on either side as he scowled up at the rapidly darkening sky. The empty swings on either side of him squeaked as the breeze pushed them, eerie in the deserted park. Clouds rolled in to cover the setting sun. He shivered as the cold wind picked up, blowing his too-long hair into his eyes. He flipped his head to unsuccessfully move his bangs away from his face, then jumped off the swing and turned toward home.

His jacket was too small and not close to warm enough for the January temperatures, especially in weather like this. He preferred freezing to death over going home, though. But he tromped in that direction anyway. A gust of wind knocked something out of a tree ahead. As Carter neared the object, a high-pitched chirping could be heard over the coming storm. He stopped, looking down at a bird's nest containing two small, brown-feathered baby birds. Carter smiled, thinking he would take it home to show Cody. As he bent to pick it up, another idea slammed into his mind with the force of a supermassive black hole explosion, overpowering any other thoughts. Carter straightened and his smile turned from innocent to raving mad as he raised his foot and stomped on the nest as hard as he could.

In slow motion, he dropped to his knees, no longer feeling the cold as heat spread from his chest, to his face, and out to his hands. He nudged the nest with his fingers and the two small occupants fell out onto the dirt path. One lay motionless, and Carter's eyes swept past it like it didn't exist. He zoned in on the second bird, his vision blurring around it as the creature emitted a pitiful squeak and flopped around like it was engaged in a wrestling match with an invisible opponent.

Carter's breaths came faster as he picked it up, cradling it in the palm of his hand. "Oh, there's a little crack in your beak. That must hurt." He squeezed the bird in his right hand and pinched its beak between a finger and thumb of his left, snapping it, then ripping it completely off with a quick motion. The squeaking reached a crescendo and Carter squeezed harder as the bird's heart raced against his palm.

Completely unaware of his surroundings, including the pelting rain that had started falling, he opened his hand and, with the slow precision of a practiced artist, Carter ripped the bird's wings from its body one at a time. Laughter bubbled up from deep within him as he repeated the act on the creature's legs, then set it on the path and watched as it flailed its body in helpless throes of pain and panic.

Carter crouched there until the baby bird stopped squawking, stopped moving, stopped living. The warmth evaporated from his body and he was surprised that he was now soaking wet, and cold from the rain he hadn't noticed until now. He kicked the nest and the two dead birds off the path, held his jacket closed at his chest, and walked home, his steps lighter and mind clearer than ever before.

TEN

PRESENT DAY
Dr. Graves

The stack of files in Chief Billings' arms made Dr. Graves wonder what he'd gotten himself into. What he and Kat had gotten themselves into.

"Must be awful slow here in the morgue for you to volunteer to search through this pile." Chief Billings plopped the files on his desk.

"Not slow," he answered. "We'll be doing a lot of this on our own time. I just want to help where I can with this case."

"And I appreciate it. It was a smart idea to check the history of that old house."

Dr. Graves raised his eyebrows. "What did you find out?"

"I have a list of previous owners. When Pup and Davis finish looking into the surgical centers, we'll cross check the lists."

"Can I have a copy of that list of owners? Just in case I find something here?"

"Sure thing." She cracked her neck, pulling her head from one side to the other. "I'll email that over to you as soon as I get back to my office."

"Thanks. And—"

"I know. I know." She waved her hands in front of her. "It isn't good to pop my neck. It could cause some kind of rare stroke."

Dr. Graves nodded.

"Old habits are hard to break." She waved before she shut his door behind her.

He pulled the top file down on the desk in front of him and flipped it open. "Why do they always put the crime scene pictures first?" he mumbled.

Someone knocked softly on his door, then pushed it open a crack. "Dr. Graves?"

"Come in, Kat. I don't know why Tracey shut my door when she left. Maybe I looked like I needed some privacy."

"Or a nap. You look tired."

"So do you. Have a seat." He gestured to the chair in front of his desk.

Kat sighed as she sat. "The mortuary picked up Mrs. Smith." She laid the signed paperwork on his desk, minus the carbon copy that went with the mortuary.

"Do we have any pending cases I've forgotten about?" He never forgot about pending cases. He wasn't sure why he asked that.

"No, thank goodness."

"Well, I guess we can get started looking through these files. You can take a stack to your office if you want." He looked over the pile at her and shrugged. "Or you could stay in here so we can bounce ideas off each other."

She smiled. Dr. Graves was learning to appreciate that smile more and more each day.

"I'll stay in here," she said. "We work better as a team."

His arms felt lighter as he handed her half the pile. He rearranged things so she could scoot her chair closer and share the top of his desk.

Kat opened the first file and grimaced. "What should we be looking for?"

"Let's focus on body type of the victim first. Set aside those who are men, young to middle age, with a larger build—let's say, five-foot-ten and over—and muscular. When we have that pile ready, we can talk about what we should look closer for."

"Good plan." She held a file up. "What about gunshot wounds?

Should we rule those out or add them to the 'investigate further' pile if the victim meets the criteria?"

"Good question." He thought for a moment. "I agree that those are unlikely related to our killer, but let's keep them for now."

Kat nodded and tossed the file in the "to keep" pile.

They got into a rhythm, and the rejected pile grew. They both jumped when Dr. Graves' phone rang. "Dr. Graves, Medical Examiner," he answered.

"Hey, Graves." Fitzpatrick's voice sounded in his ear.

"*Doctor* Graves," he corrected impatiently.

"Sorry. Dr. Graves, we have a case for you. It doesn't appear to be a homicide, but it did occur during or after a drunken party at a motel, so it qualifies as an M.E. case."

"Okay..."

"I just wanted to let you know the body's on its way. Davis and I will be shortly behind, we need to go print the scene pictures out for you."

"Oh, goody. I can't wait," Dr. Graves said.

"Was that sarcasm, Dr. Graves? I don't believe I've ever heard that from you before." Fitzpatrick laughed. "Maybe there is hope for your sense of humor after all."

The doctor hung up with a scowl.

Kat had already stood.

"They're bringing in a suspicious death."

She was halfway to the door. "I'll go get setup."

"Thanks, Kat. You're invaluable."

"I know." She flashed a smile as she walked out the door.

—⟀—

KAT PREPARED to draw blood from the deceased's femoral vein while Dr. Graves stood with the detectives.

"So," Dr. Graves said, "let me make sure I'm understanding this correctly. The deceased was at a party. Witnesses say that he got really drunk—or 'wasted' as you put it—came out of the bathroom exclaiming that something was hanging down in the back of his throat. He retrieved a hemostat from a fishing tackle box that he kept in his truck and proceeded to try removing the perceived foreign body from his throat, getting it to his lips multiple times but never able to actually remove it." He looked at the detectives for confirmation.

"Yes," Davis said. "You got it."

Dr. Graves nodded. "And then, he either fell asleep or passed out on one of the beds. When one of the witnesses tried to wake him up late this morning"—he looked at his watch—"or early afternoon, the witness found that he had expired sometime within the last eight to ten hours."

"Exactly." Fitzpatrick grinned and slapped the doctor on the arm. "You get all the weird ones." He shook his head, still grinning.

"Yes." Dr. Graves frowned. "You've mentioned that before."

"Come on, Pup," Davis said. "We need to go finish up with those surgical centers. The chief will tan our hides if we don't finish up today."

The detectives left and Kat said, "I've always wondered, why do they call Fitzpatrick 'Pup'?"

Dr. Graves put on his gown and mask, then started pulling his gloves on. "When he was a rookie his T.O. said he looked like a poor, pitiful little puppy and started calling him 'Patty Pup,' later shortened to just 'Pup.' The name stuck."

"T.O.?"

"Training Officer." Dr. Graves stepped up to the deceased and pried his mouth open. "Shine the overhead light in here." He reached in with a pair of forceps and pulled something pink and meaty out of the deceased's throat. And it was still attached to the soft palate. "Holy Darwin," he exclaimed.

"What is that?" Kat asked.

"Take a look for yourself." He pulled it further, careful not to stretch the already stretched tissue. The tip of it reached the man's lips.

Kat leaned in and gasped. "Is...is that...his *uvula?*"

"Yes. Very good."

"What in the hell..."

Pulling the microscope lenses over, he examined it closely, turning it around to look at all angles. He straightened and pushed the hands-free microscope out of the way. "My educated guess: he consumed alcohol beyond his capacity for average or even below average intelligence, saw his uvula in the back of his throat where it's supposed to be, thought it looked like something that didn't belong there, and spent the next hour trying to remove it using hemostats he retrieved from his fishing box."

Kat shook her head, her eyes wide. Her mouth was probably open too, but he couldn't tell because she was wearing a surgical mask.

"He gave up, then passed out on his back. Two things happened, the uvula swelled up from the trauma he inflicted upon it, and it was stretched out far beyond it's normal length. It was sucked down into his trachea when he took a breath, thus blocking his airway and asphyxiating him."

"Holy Darwin is right," Kat said.

"Get some soft tissue x-rays of his throat and neck to make sure there wasn't really a foreign body in there, then take some pictures." He flipped his gloves off into the biohazard bin. "I'm not even going to open him up, the cause of death is obvious."

"Should I still send the blood?"

"Yes, I'm sure the police will want to know his EtOH level."

She printed a sticker and ripped it off the small printer next to the computer. Affixing the label to the blood sample, she said, "How do you even categorize something like this?"

Dr. Graves sighed. "Accidental, because 'lacking judgment' isn't a choice."

WITH THE PHONE pressed between his shoulder and ear, Dr. Graves shuffled through one of the unsolved murder files while he waited for Chief Billings to come to the phone.

"Hey, Dean." She breathed heavily, the sound whooshing in his ear.

"Hello, Tracey. Is everything okay?"

"Yeah, fine. Just rushing around this afternoon. What's up?"

After explaining his autopsy results to the chief, Dr. Graves asked, "Do your detectives purposefully assign me the bizarre cases?"

Tracey laughed. "No, Dean, they do not. I think you must have a hex on you or something. Maybe you should look around your office for a hidden hex bag."

"You watch too much *Supernatural*," he muttered.

"No such thing as too much *Supernatural*," she said. "I have to go. Let me know if you find anything worthwhile in those records."

"I will." He hung up.

Kat entered his office and sat opposite him, grabbed a file from the top of the pile, and started looking through it silently.

It was well past their usual quitting time when they got through the whole pile. Dr. Graves moved the larger stack of files—victims who didn't match the profile—and left the smaller stack on his desk. He leaned back in his chair, running his hands through his messy hair. "Well, I'm going to stay a little longer and dig into these files. You don't need to stay, though. I'm sure you have better things to do on a fine Thursday evening."

She sighed. "Sadly, no, I don't have anything better to do." She grabbed a file from the top and opened it. "What are we looking for this time?"

"First, I'm going to order a pizza; I need to refuel. Is pepperoni all right?"

"Pepperoni is more than all right."

That brought a smile to his lips. It was the only kind of pizza he would eat. After calling in the order, with instructions to leave it with the security guard upstairs, he grabbed a pen and notebook. "Okay. What details should we be looking for?'"

Kat scrunched one side of her face up as she thought. "Method of the murder? See if any drugs were used or similar maiming?"

He wrote her suggestions down, then checked his email. He printed off the list of previous owners for the abandoned house the killer had used. He was a little surprised that Tracey had remembered to send the list, as frazzled as she'd seemed on the phone. "And this." He pulled two copies off the printer behind his desk and handed one of them to Kat. "See if we can see any connections to any of these people—including witnesses, neighbors... anyone that was questioned in the initial investigation."

They spent the next two hours eating pizza and searching murder files.

And found exactly nothing helpful.

Dr. Graves threw the last file onto the discard pile with a deep exhale. "Well, I was hoping to find something, but not expecting to, so I suppose I shouldn't be disappointed."

He stood and offered his hand to Kat to help her stand. "It's late. Let me walk you to your car." He'd said that to her every time they'd worked late over the last year and a half, but somehow it felt different this time. The smile that made her eyes sparkle seemed different, too. More intense somehow. He swallowed, slow to release her hand once she'd stood.

Clearing his throat, he turned toward the door, then waited for Kat to walk through before turning the lights off and closing and locking it. He held his arm out for her to hold to as he had done dozens of times. The first time, she'd commented on how old-fashioned he was...and how that was something she appreciated. He shot a quick glance at her and smiled. As young as she was, she was an old soul, like him.

"I was thinking about something you said the other day," she said as they stepped into the elevator. "If the 'first kill' of a serial killer is usually someone they know, and they want to keep it personal and to themselves, maybe who we need to look for is not an unsolved murder victim, but a missing person."

"Yes." That's exactly where his thoughts had taken him. "That should be our next step. I'll return the homicide files to the precinct tomorrow and ask Tracey to have some missing person files pulled for us."

They left the elevator on the main floor and walked in silence to Kat's car. Dr. Graves waited until she was seated and buckled in. "I'll see you in the morning," he said, wanting to linger a little even though it was late.

"I'll be here." She put her key in the ignition and looked up at him. "Thanks for the pizza."

"Thank you for helping with this fishing expedition I've started."

"Any time."

He closed her door and stepped back, watching as she drove away, before going to his own car.

Kat has pretty eyes. He climbed into his car. *Wonder why I never noticed before.*

ELEVEN

Present Day
Carter, Age 28

Carter told himself he was done. And he meant it. He wasn't crazy. He'd had a job to do and he'd done it; revenge had been served.

He looked again at the open med cart in front of him, then at the nurse tending to the post-op patient. He slipped a vial of rocuronium into his lab coat pocket, then a second one for good measure.

Just in case.

He didn't *plan* to need it, but one never knows. He'd grab more intubation supplies tomorrow at the new surgical center. Best to spread it out. Less noticeable that way. And he'd pick up some syringes and IV stuff at the plastic surgeon's office on Friday.

Heat burned in his chest as the memory of pleading screams floated into his mind. He gave himself a few seconds to enjoy it before shaking his head and whispering, "No. I'm done."

But you never know.

—ᐯ—

Standing next to his car, pumping gas, Carter perked up as a man and a young boy exited the convenience store, the man carrying an eighteen-pack of beer. The boy looked down as he walked, sniffling like he was trying not to cry.

The man yelled, "Stop your whimpering!" He smacked the boy's head hard enough to make him stumble.

Red rage slammed over Carter's vision, and by the time he could see again, the man and boy had pulled out of the parking lot.

An explosion of thought detonated in his mind as his breath came faster than his lungs had room for.

I will find the next man deserving of my justice.

He closed his eyes and pictured the man with the beer strapped to a table, begging for mercy. A feeling of great relief spread through Carter, and he smiled.

I guess I'm not done after all.

⎓⌁

"Ahh, dude! That game was a bummer. Let me buy you a drink to drown your sorrows." Carter wasn't the only one to offer, so it wasn't suspicious. He had been watching the stringy-haired drunk all week in this crappy bar—it wasn't the asshole from the gas station, but it was close enough. Carter smiled into his diet soda.

He'd known this man was his next target by the second night, when he'd heard the drunk grumbling about having to pay child support. About how he'd never even wanted "the brat" to begin with. The next night sealed the deal, when the jerk had answered his phone and snarled into it, "I don't care if it's my night. I'm not coming. Just tell the kid something came up."

Carter had watched with growing rage as the drunk ended the call then turned his phone off before returning it to his greasy pocket.

Tonight was the night. An hour after the stupid game ended, the guy was sufficiently inebriated and ready to be reaped. Carter made sure to leave first, like last time, then waited for the staggering loser to exit the bar alone. He chuckled to himself at how easy it was to get these losers to willingly get into his car that looked nothing like a taxi.

⎓⌁

KILLING a man in a cemetery added to Carter's excitement. A soon-to-be dead person begging for his life surrounded by already-dead people was paradoxical in the most profound way. But the public location meant that Carter had to figure out a way to keep his victim quiet without spoiling his own fun. There was always a chance that someone could be lurking nearby, visiting the grave of a loved-one or just being macabre.

Carter spread the man's jaws open with the laryngoscope and wedged a bite block between his top and bottom teeth. He needed to do something different before intubating the guy this time. He grinned as the light from the scope illuminated the vocal folds. With two quick slices of the scalpel, he fixed the noise problem. Knowing the drunk could feel every slice made Carter giddy.

He pulled out the tube after a good twenty minutes of surgical artwork; the paralytic was wearing off and the drunk could breathe on his own now.

The drunk's face flushed with the effort to scream. His neck veins bulged. His horrified, protruding eyes as he croaked out barely audible pleas to Carter...

Carter worried that he'd miss the screaming, but instead, the overall effect of the whispered pain and terror drew him in.

TWELVE

PRESENT DAY
Dr. Graves

Sunday afternoon bloomed warm and beautiful, and Dr. Graves took full advantage of the blossoming flowers in his backyard. It had been a quiet weekend, thankfully. He and Kat found nothing of interest in the missing persons files the previous week, so that had been a disappointment, but he'd asked Chief Billings to send any new reports along.

He dabbed his brush in the rose gold color he'd mixed on the palette and touched it gently to his canvas, determined to get the flower's petals just right. His phone buzzed in his pocket and his concentration—and his hand—slipped, ruining the flower he'd been working on for the last fifteen minutes.

"Happy little accident my rear, Bob Ross," he growled as he set the palette down and dug in his pocket for his phone.

Before he could even speak, Detective Fitzpatrick's voice blared in his ear. "Graves, we've got another one."

"*Doctor* Graves. And, another *what*?" Aggravation seeped from his gut to his vocal cords.

"Uhh...sorry...yeah, Dr. Graves," Fitzpatrick stuttered. "Another murder victim. Like the last one. Can you come to the scene?"

Dr. Graves wiped his hands on his apron and scowled at a butterfly flapping lazily by. "Yes. What's the address?"

"Magnolia Cemetery. In a crypt. You'll see where we are when you get here."

On his way to the scene, Dr. Graves called Kat. "Hi, Kat, it's Dr. Graves."

"Yes," she said, a tease in her voice, "I know your voice and your phone number. What's up?"

"Are you up for a little overtime? I could use your help at the M.E. Office in a couple of hours."

"Uh oh. That doesn't sound good. What's going on?" The strained tone in her voice told him she already had a good idea what he was going to say.

"He struck again. We have another victim. I'm on my way to the scene."

"Damn it. I'll meet you at the morgue." She hung up.

$-\wedge-$

THERE WAS no question as to where the body was. Police cars and CSI vans lined the small lane closest to the crypt in question.

Dr. Graves stepped slowly into the small stone building, taking it all in. The setup was much the same—except that instead of a table, the victim was strapped to the top of a very plain sarcophagus. The doctor avoided stepping on the small splashes of blood that decorated the cement floor.

Again, the killer had left the ET tube neatly beside the victim's head, and the IV remained in his arm. This victim was of the same build as the first: at least six-feet tall, with broad shoulders.

The doctor examined the body, walking all the way around it. "He's escalated. I didn't think he could escalate from what he did to the first man, but...he proved me wrong."

The victim's intestines had been pulled through a small, precise incision in his lower abdomen and left to hang off the side of the body to the floor, still attached. The other visible injuries were similar to the first victim. Blood trickled from his ears, viscous fluid from his punctured eyeballs.

"How did the killer get him in here without being seen? The

gates are closed and locked at eight o'clock. This crypt would have been locked." Dr. Graves looked from Davis to Fitzpatrick.

"Preliminary findings suggest that he may have used a wheelchair to get the victim from his vehicle to the crypt," Davis explained. "CSI is investigating the tracks. The perp picked the locks to the gate and the crypt. According to the manager here, it would have had to be between two and three A.M.; that's when the night guard takes his break."

Dr. Graves studied the body again. "The oldest of these lacerations and bruises look to be three days old at most. He didn't keep this one alive as long."

Fitzpatrick nodded. "We figured that he rushed this one because it wasn't as secure of a spot as the house had been. He would have had to keep the victim quiet, and he would likely have had to stay here the whole time." He gestured to one corner where a pile of discarded food wrappers lay, and another corner where a five-gallon bucket stood, half full of urine and feces.

"Well..." Dr. Graves grimaced. "The killer is obviously not worried about us finding his DNA. Which likely means he's not in the criminal justice system."

"That's what we thought," Fitzpatrick said. "How would he have been able to keep this man quiet? You said with the last one that he allowed the medication to wear off so he could watch the victim's reaction." The detective looked down at the tortured remains. "That would not have been quiet."

Dr. Graves put a pair of gloves on and pried the victim's mouth open. "Shine your light in here, detective."

Fitzpatrick did as requested, and the doctor peered inside and shook his head. "Looks like he cut this man's vocal folds. He could have pushed all the air his lungs could hold out through his throat, and all that would be heard was silent screams. The whoosh of air."

"That's just..." Davis covered his throat with a hand. "Brutal."

Picking up the ET tube, Dr. Graves inspected it closer. "This is a different brand than the last one. Check with the medical supply companies in the state and see if they can tell you which surgical centers and hospitals use which brands."

"Okay," Davis said. "That might help us narrow down all the names we got from our surgical center search. They pretty much all use per diem anesthetists. If we can rule some of them out, it would make life easier."

Turning to one of the crime scene techs, Dr. Graves asked, "When will you be done here?"

"We're wrapping up now. Should be ready to bag him in twenty minutes."

"I'll head over to the morgue then. Detectives, I assume I'll see you there?"

They nodded.

He removed his gloves and placed them in the discard bag that had been set up outside the crypt. His mind spun in multiple different directions on his way to the M.E. office.

—⋀—

"Send blood and plasma for the same labs as before and add a PEth to the whole-blood sample." Dr. Graves' jaw was tight and his head pounded like a bass drum. He rubbed his temples.

Kat nodded, added the order into the computer, labeled the blood samples, and left to send them off to the lab.

When she came back, she handed Dr. Graves two acetaminophen tablets and a bottle of water.

"Thank you." He frowned. "How did you know I needed this?"

She rolled her eyes. "How long have we worked together? I know when you have a headache."

He couldn't find it in himself to smile, but he nodded and took the pills.

"What is PEth?" Kat asked. "I don't remember ordering that before."

"It's phosphatidylethanol, an alcohol metabolite. It's a biomarker of drinking habits, sort of like a hemoglobin $A1C$ is for glucose levels. It's concentrated in whole blood and will tell us if this man was a heavy drinker."

"So, that would give us one more thing to add to the list of the killer's 'type' of victim? Because the first one was a heavy drinker."

"Exactly." He took a deep breath. "Well, let's get started. It's going to be a long night."

THIRTEEN

Fourteen Years Ago
Carter, age 14

Carter stepped through the door on high alert. Dick-wad's truck was in the driveway. He'd taken to skipping work two or three times a week. No way he'd still have a job if he didn't work for his brother. He'd kicked the drinking up a notch in the last couple of years. Beer was just an appetizer now; whiskey was the main course, the dessert...and the evening snack...and the late-night snack.

"I told you not to eat those chips, you little asshole!"

Carter dropped his backpack in the doorway and rushed to the kitchen, rounding the corner just as Dick-wad raised his fist before a cowering Cody. Carter slid to a stop between them, pushing Cody behind him. Carter had grown over the last couple of years, but The Dick still towered over him.

"I ate them!" he blurted out, even though he didn't. He didn't even know what chips the psycho was talking about. He'd probably hidden them and couldn't remember where, or he'd already eaten the blasted things.

He narrowed his eyes suspiciously at Carter. "You little shit!" Dick-wad lurched forward and pushed him. He landed hard on the tile floor, the jolt running from his tailbone all the way to his teeth. Cody had jumped out of the way just in time.

Carter looked at his brother and nodded toward the door. Cody hesitated only a half-second before high-tailing it out of there, probably heading to his friend's house down the street.

His favorite punching bag leaving took the wind out of Dick-wad's sails, and he had to satisfy himself with a kick to Carter's thigh. The teen didn't even flinch, even though his muscle cramped into a Charley horse with the blow. He waited until The Dick wandered into the other room before he released his held breath and stretched his leg out to get rid of the cramp.

FOURTEEN

Present Day

Dr. Graves

Wednesday evening, Dr. Graves relaxed in an Adirondack chair on his back porch, a light spring breeze causing the temperature to cool just enough to be pleasant. He sipped his cream soda and tried to convince himself that waiting two weeks for lab results wasn't really going to slow the investigation down. The detectives were following other leads.

He set the glass on the small table next to him and breathed in deep. His sleep cycle was never going to get back to normal if he continued to have seven-hour autopsies that carried on late into the night—or early morning, as it were. That had been Sunday into Monday, and he still hadn't recovered completely.

A loping Golden Retriever headed straight for the porch from the neighbor's yard.

Dr. Graves scowled. "Winston! No! Go home!"

As usual, the furry mutt ignored him, jumped up the three steps to the porch, and sat at the doctor's feet, a quiet little whine coming from the back of the dog's throat.

Dr. Graves fought to keep the scowl on his face and the gruff in his voice. "Fine. I'll pet you. But it doesn't mean I like you." As soon as his hand moved toward the dog's ears, Winston laid his head in the doctor's lap, leaning up against his legs. "Don't you dare tell anyone about this, Winston."

The dog's soft fur in his hand and the warmth of his head laying on the doctor's lap lulled him into a more relaxed state than he'd been in for weeks. He leaned back and closed his eyes. The serenity only lasted a few minutes, though. Winston wasn't one to sit idle for long. He pulled back and licked the doctor's hand, whining a little louder this time.

"No licking," Dr. Graves said in a stern voice that softened as he stood. "Fine. I'll go get you a treat. But again, this is just between us. Remember—I don't like dogs."

After scarfing down the dog treat, Winston gave a low bark and headed back to his own yard.

"Good," Dr. Graves said. "Go home where you belong." He returned to his seat and had just lifted his cream soda to his lips when the dog came trotting back and dropped a dirty, dog-slobbery tennis ball at his feet. If dogs could smile, Winston's face was how it would look as he stood and wagged his tail with gusto.

Dr. Graves rolled his eyes and set his drink back on the table. "Fine. I'll play with you." He looked down at the nasty ball. "But I'm going to put gloves on first."

The mindless game of fetch loosened the tension in his shoulders and even brought a few quiet laughs to the lips of the doctor. For a while, he was able to put the serial killer's repulsive murders out of his mind.

"Winston!" the neighbor, Amy, called for her dog as she made her way into the doctor's yard. "I'm so sorry, Dr. Graves. I hope he didn't bother you much."

He handed the slobber-soaked tennis ball to her and tried to replace the earlier scowl on his face, the success of which was about a one on a scale of one to ten. "Well, he is rather annoying." He pulled off the nitrile gloves and wadded them into a ball, noting the small twitch at the corners of Amy's mouth.

He wasn't fooling her. They'd had this same discussion many times over the last three years since Winston had first come calling. He still needed to keep up the charade; wouldn't want anyone to think he'd gone soft.

His façade was broken, however, as he leaned down to scratch the dog behind the ears. "See you later, Winston."

Amy winked and turned, and Winston followed her home.

Dr. Graves watched them. "Dumb dog," he whispered with a smile.

—⋀—

"Yesterday must have been a slow day for mysterious deaths, seeing as how we have nothing to do today...except catch up." Kat leaned on Dr. Graves' open doorway.

"Indeed, it was." He looked up from his computer screen and smiled.

Kat took that as an invitation to come in and sit down. "Do you have any fun plans for this weekend?"

He pushed the screen to the side so he could maintain eye contact as they interacted. "Well, I decided I need to do a little relaxing after the month we've had, so I'm going to go fishing."

Kat's eyes widened, and she leaned forward almost imperceptibly. "Oh? Where?"

Raising an eyebrow, Dr. Graves answered, "Clark's Hill."

"You mean Strom Thurmond Lake?" Her smile looked like pure mischief.

"Hmf," he grumbled. "My dad always called it Clark's Hill, so that's what I call it. Whoever came up with the idea to name stuff after politicians?"

Kat laughed. "Politicians did."

A low, quick chuckle released itself from somewhere inside him. "Good point."

"Is this meant to be a solitary day of fishing," Kat asked, "or would you like some company?"

His heart skipped a beat—he'd have to go in for his physical soon, maybe request an ECG. "That depends entirely on the company."

"Well..." She looked down at her hands. "I could use a little relaxing myself. And I love to fish..."

"There are plenty of great places to fish nearby, what kind..." He stopped as her left eyebrow arched to her hairline. "Oh...you meant you'd like to come fishing with *me*."

See, intellectual introverts could learn new things.

"Yes, Dr. Graves." She smiled. "If you'd like my company on your fishing trip tomorrow, I'd love to join you. I have a license and my own gear."

His mouth decided to produce an extra dose of saliva at that moment, and Dr. Graves had a hard time selecting which words he wanted to use to answer her. "Well...yes...that would be"—should he say 'lovely,' 'wonderful,' 'amazing'?— "great. Really great." Maybe he was having a mini-stroke.

"Are you sure?" Kat's eyebrows dropped down into a questioning wave. "You seem kind of hesitant. I don't want to crash your party if you don't want any company. Or my company specifically."

"No, no." His stomach flipped. Medical school hadn't been able to explain why one's insides did such things when confronted with... the opposite sex. It had only happened to him rarely; he couldn't even remember the last time...high school, probably. "I'd really love to have you along. I will pick you up at six tomorrow morning." His brain had finally re-engaged.

Her smile strangely coincided with another flip of his stomach. "Six A.M. it is," Kat said. "Do you remember where I live?" He'd once given her a ride home when her car was in the shop.

"Indeed, I do." A sudden thought struck him. "I'll pack us a lunch." This eating together thing was becoming a habit.

"And I'll bring some snacks and water."

Dr. Graves had a hard time concentrating for the rest of the day.

FIFTEEN

The 4Runner idled as Carter stared at the old elementary school set to be demolished in a few weeks. *His* old elementary school. Dick-wad's. He nodded, a grim smile touching his lips as he looked down at the old class photo in his hand. Little *Richard* stood on the back row, a toothless grin on his freckled face.

This was the perfect location for his next act of retribution. Carter needed to stay connected to Dick-wad while he avenged his mom and Cody—so the universe would know where the credit should go.

I'm like a superhero. Others were starting to see the change in him, too. He was sure of it. The nurses flirted with him like crazy now. He'd already found a new bar with a new drunk to abolish. He planned to approach this one, gain his trust. This time, the drunk would go with him willingly. Of course, he wouldn't know what awaited him when he got into Carter's car. He'd just think he made friends with a superhero.

SIXTEEN

Present Day

Dr. Graves

A few thin clouds rolled overhead in the early light as Dr. Graves pulled up to the curb outside Kat's quaint bungalow. He put the car in park and got out, but before he could make his way up the walk, Kat stepped out the door. Her arms were loaded down with a fishing pole and tackle box, and she had a bag slung over one shoulder, pulling a small, rolling cooler behind her. He reached her as she struggled with her keys, trying to lock the door.

She glanced at him with a smirk. "Nice hat."

"It keeps the sun off my face." He moved to take her fishing pole. "Let me take some of that."

"I've got it." She dropped her keys, then knocked the old-school tackle box against a rocking chair on her porch, and it sprang open, dumping most of the contents stored in the top drawer. "Damn it!" Kat dropped everything, then snatched her keys from the beautifully-treated wooden planks and used them to lock the door. "Sorry about the profanity."

"No need to apologize. It doesn't bother me...very much." He bent down and started picking up the hooks and lures and bobbers with a careful hand.

Kat snort-laughed and joined in the cleanup.

Five minutes later, they were on their way.

After driving down multiple dirt roads, then hiking a half-mile through thick forest, they were able to find an out-of-the-way area that opened up to a small, sandy beach. Dr. Graves set up the two fishing chairs he'd packed in and watched in awe while Kat prepared her fishing rod. She tied on a sinker and a Rapala with the skill of a professional bass fisher.

She looked up at him as he gawked. "You'd better get your pole ready. Didn't I tell you this is a competition?"

"Oh, is it now?" He raised an eyebrow.

"Of course. I was raised with four brothers; everything is a competition." She stood, stepped closer to the shoreline, and cast a perfect arc out over the smooth waters of the lake. She let her line sink to the bottom before closing the bail, then she reeled a little to remove the slack, jerked up a couple of times, then reeled in at just the right speed to set the lure spinning.

"Hmm," the doctor said. "I suppose I'd better get started then." The sun glinting off the soft blonde highlights in her otherwise brunette hair reminded him of Angel Amber Kiss Pansies, and distracted him momentarily.

Just as he raised his arm to cast, Kat got a strong hit, jerked up on her pole, and started reeling faster. Dr. Graves shook his head with a smile, cast out into the lake, and set his pole down just in time to watch Kat pull a good-sized bass onto the shore.

She held it up beside her. "Take a picture!" She beamed as he snapped a photo with his phone. "Catch and release, right?" she said as she removed the hook with a pair of hemostats.

"Of course." He watched her release the fish back into the lake. "I don't eat fish anyway."

Kat rolled her eyes. "Of course you don't."

They each ended up catching three fish by mid-morning, though, according to Kat's ever-changing rules, she was winning the "contest" based on size.

Fishing slowed down as the morning wore on and the sun reflected off the dark water.

Dr. Graves tilted his head back and closed his eyes, enjoying the warmth of the day before the humidity would make it too unbearable.

He heard Kat moving around, but wasn't curious enough to see what she was doing to open his eyes...until a small splash of water hit his face.

He sat forward so fast he knocked his pole to the ground.

Kat stood ankle deep in the lake, laughing as she splashed more water his way. The water glistened on her tone, tan legs where she'd folded up her jeans. He should probably remind her that too much sunlight causes skin cancer. Instead, he stood, tried to look grouchy but his smiling face wouldn't cooperate, and stepped toward her.

Holding her hands up, palms toward him, Kat took two steps back, still laughing. The third step ended with her tumbling backwards, arms wind-milling, into the water, completely immersed.

Must be a drop-off there. Just as his brain kicked in to worry mode, she surfaced, spitting as she tread water. It was Dr. Graves' turn to laugh. And laugh he did, harder than he had for as long as he could remember. He bent over with his hands on his knees, the laughter now turned to more of a wheezing sound as his vocal cords and lungs rebelled against the unfamiliar blasts of mirth. He gained control of himself as Kat pulled herself up the shelf she'd obviously fallen off of. He wiped the tears from his cheeks and slipped his shoes off before stepping into the shallow water to help her to her feet.

An impish grin appeared on her face as she grasped his hand... and pulled him into the abyss.

Dr. Graves pushed off the bottom and kicked up toward the shadow of his floating hat above. The lake wasn't very deep there, maybe a couple of feet over his head. He burst up out of the water, launching his chest up onto the shelf. He grabbed Kat's ankle and pulled her in beside him.

An epic splash-battle ensued. It was obvious to Dr. Graves that Kat was not a newbie at this sport as he was. He couldn't remember ever even swimming in a natural body of water—they carried too many infectious organisms. All these thoughts flew from his mind as Kat put her hands on his shoulders and lifted herself out of the water, dunking him under in the process.

With the speed of a cheetah, she launched herself onto the shelf, to her feet, and out of the water. She stood dripping and laughing as Dr. Graves swam out to get his hat that had drifted several yards away. By the time he got back to the shore and up onto land again, she'd spread out the blanket she'd packed to eat lunch on. Kat laid down on one side, leaving room for him to recline beside her as they let the warm sun dry them. The smallish blanket left his legs from the knees down positioned in the dirt. But that barely registered, as all he could think about was Kat's arm resting lightly against his, distracting him in a purely pleasant way.

After sufficiently drying the front, Kat flipped over onto her stomach and laid her head on her folded arms. Dr. Graves followed suit, only he gently turned over instead of flipping. Soon they were both raised up on their elbows, talking.

"How old are you, Dean?" Kat asked.

"I turned thirty-four last month. How old are you?" He'd never even thought to ask that question. She looked much younger than him, but age didn't matter when your assistant was more competent than any that had come before her.

"I am twenty-nine."

"Well," he said with surprise. "I would have guessed much younger. But I've never been very good at guessing people's ages... living people anyway."

"Yeah, I guess you can't just ask a living person to hand over a tooth for you to examine and do testing on." She smiled. "Most people guess me to be younger than I am. I think it's because I'm short."

"That's likely part of it," he said. "But you also have very young-looking skin. It's so smooth, and your eyes still sparkle like you haven't lived long enough to lose hope in humanity."

Kat touched his arm. "I do believe you just gave me a compliment, Dr. Graves. I'm going to mark this day down in my calendar." She squeezed his arm, then moved her hand away. "I might even try to convince myself that you were flirting with me, even though I know that's not the case."

His eyes widened. "I"—he cleared his throat—"I...didn't...or, wasn't..." He looked away, examining a rock out in front of him. "I was only stating the facts."

"I know." Even though he wasn't looking at her, he could hear the smile in her voice. "But it sure is fun to see the always-steady Dr. Graves get flustered once in a while."

He lowered his head, hiding it in his folded arms, the one she'd touched still tingling. "If you want to think I was flirting..." His voice was muffled, hidden away in the safety of his arm-cocoon. "It's okay with me."

In the silence that ensued, Dr. Graves chastised himself for allowing a moment of spontaneity to emerge. Was Kat upset at what he'd said? It had been very unprofessional. He dared a peek over at her.

She raised her eyebrows and smiled. Or was it a smirk? He couldn't tell. But it made her eyes light up, so it didn't really matter—it was a beautiful sight to behold.

She laughed and pushed his shoulder, rocking his cocoon. He smiled and sat up, reached for his backpack, and said, "Let's eat lunch. I'm hungry."

Mid-lunch, which consisted of peanut butter and jelly sandwiches on whole wheat, baked chips, and carrot sticks, they were interrupted by a park ranger.

"Hello," the ranger said as he stepped through the trees onto the sand. "It looks like you two have found a nice secluded spot." His eyes roved over the fishing gear and back to Dr. Graves' face. "I won't stay long; I just need to check your fishing licenses."

"No problem." Dr. Graves grabbed his backpack and unzipped a small pocket on the side. He pulled out his wallet, flipped it open, retrieved his license, and handed it to the ranger.

He didn't know where Kat had been keeping her license, but she beat him to it. The ranger already held hers in his hand. He smiled down at her. "Well, Katherine—"

"Call me Kat, please," she interrupted with a smile.

"Of course, Kat. It looks like everything is up to par." He handed it back and switched to inspecting Dr. Graves' license. He raised an eyebrow and frowned. "Dr. Graves?"

"Yes?"

His frown turned back into a smile, but not the same one he'd given to Kat. "I didn't recognize you with that hat on...or those casual clothes." He gestured to Dr. Graves' jeans. "Do you remember me?"

Dr. Graves straightened and squinted up at the man. "Didn't we work on a case together? A couple of years ago?"

His smile widened. "Yes, we did!"

"It's Marty, isn't it?"

Marty nodded then switched gears and shook his head. "That was one strange case..."

Kat leaned back on an elbow. "Most of his are."

"Yeah..." Dr. Graves said slowly. "I think I'm cursed."

Marty laughed. "Well, that may be, but I was totally impressed that you figured out the guy died while noodling, at night, while intoxicated."

"Noodling?" Kat asked.

The ranger rolled his eyes. "It's when rednecks catch catfish with their hands."

"Oh, yeah, I've heard of that," Kat said.

Marty squatted down next to their heads—eliciting a totally involuntary scowl from Dr. Graves—and said, "Yeah, we found this body washed up on the shore of a river. He'd been reported missing the day before."

Kat looked around Marty to make eye contact with Dr. Graves. "How did you know he'd been *noodling*?"

He smiled. "The cardiform teeth marks on his arm—they aren't really teeth, though, not sure why they're called that. The marks went all the way up past his elbow. He caught himself a big one." Dr.

Graves shook his head. "Or it caught him, I guess. Pulled him under and drowned him."

—⋀—

Dr. Graves pulled up to Kat's house and jumped out before she could protest. "Let me help you carry all this stuff."

She stared at him for a few seconds then smiled wryly. "Okay."

He followed her up the walk and waited while she fumbled with her keys again. As he set her stuff down just inside the front door, he said, "I had a wonderful time. You surprised me today on many levels, and I appreciated your company."

Kat cocked her head to the side. "In what ways did I surprise you?"

Looking down at his shoes, Dr. Graves cleared his throat, silently cursing himself for opening up the gateway for such an open-ended question. He straightened his shoulders and looked her in the eyes. "Well, you are an experienced fisherman, for one. And, you were able to make me forget about serial killers and strange deaths for several hours. And..." He paused, taking a deep breath before continuing. "You have a truly beautiful and contagious laugh. We don't get much of an opportunity in our line of work to hear each other's laughter." He willed the flush that was creeping up his neck to halt and recede.

Kat's smile faded and her eyes turned serious.

Uh oh.

She stepped closer to him and laid a hand on his arm. "I'm glad I could help you forget for a short time. It's only recently that I realized these cases truly bother you. You've always been so professional and..." She frowned. "Not *cold*...but maybe...*impervious* to the effects of so much death." The smile returned to her lips. "It's good to know you have the ability to feel and show emotions. And your laugh is amazing. I had no idea your eyes could sparkle like they did today." She gave his arm a squeeze and then let go. "See you Monday."

SEVENTEEN

Thirteen Years Ago
Carter, age 15

Clouds obscured the sun, making it seem later than five o'clock. Carter just hoped it didn't start raining until after he reached his destination. He didn't mind walking; in fact, he was pretty pleased with the strength and endurance he'd developed over the past year just by hiking everywhere. He figured there were days when he walked twenty miles just to avoid going home.

A couple of raindrops pattered against his backpack just as he reached for the door to tonight's chosen McDonald's. He ordered a small soda, counting out the change, mostly nickels and pennies, he pulled out of his pocket. His usual booth was vacant, thankfully, so he scooted into it and pulled his Geometry book out of his backpack. He should have plenty of time to finish his homework and study for Friday's biology test before they kicked him out at midnight. He'd worked hard to get good grades, figuring it was his way out. He'd also worked hard to suppress the monster impulses he sometimes had. Like the time he'd killed those birds. It hadn't been his only or last act of twisted animal abuse. But after almost getting caught with the neighbor's cat...anyhow, he didn't want to be a psycho. He could control it. And, he had controlled it for the last year. He shook his head, dispelling the dark thoughts.

Guilt and hunger gnawed at his stomach as he sipped his drink, staring at the equations he needed to memorize, but he just couldn't be at home anymore. In the same house with that drunk piece of shit. The Dick didn't even work now, he just sat home all day, drinking, while Carter's mom worked two jobs. Carter clenched his jaw.

She's just as much to blame. Frickin' coward.

Sometimes he wondered what his dad would do if he were there. But Dad was a coward, too. Carter didn't want to think about whether or not he, himself, was a coward for avoiding home almost every night. It eased his guilt to know that Cody was safe, likely. Carter would suck it up and go home after school if he thought Cody was in danger, but his little brother spent most of his time down the street from their house with his friend's family. They were Mormons. Carter was pretty sure they had to show compassion as part of their religion or something. He was just glad Cody had somewhere safe to go while their mom worked her life away. *I should still be there, for when he gets home, just in case.*

Carter shook his head. Dick-wad would likely be passed out by the time either he or Cody got home. He took another drink and worked to relax his jaw, then he forced himself to concentrate on his homework.

⌁

ELEVEN YEARS AGO

Carter, age 17

"YOUR GRADES ARE EXCELLENT, CARTER." Mrs. Crowther smiled proudly; she'd been his school counselor since he was a freshman. "It looks like the plan we made for you last year is well on its way."

Carter nodded.

"Are you still planning on going to nursing school after you graduate next year?"

He cringed. "Nursing school" sounded so wimpy. "Yeah. I've been looking into some of those accelerated programs you told me about. It looks like I can get an associate's degree in less than two years, then I can work while I get my bachelor's and hopefully be ready to apply to CRNA school soon after that."

"So, that's still the plan? To be a nurse anesthetist?"

"Heck, yeah," he said. "They make bank! And it's way quicker than going to medical school."

"Have you thought about how you're going to pay for school? Those accelerated programs can be quite pricey."

He shrugged. Yeah, he'd thought about it. He'd thought about it a lot. "From what you've told me and what I've found with my own research, I should be able to get grants. My mom's income is well below the requirement. My backup plan is student loans."

"Sounds like you've done your homework." She patted his hand. "Let me know if I can help with anything."

"Thanks." Carter slung his backpack over his shoulder and hurried outside. He had just enough time to stop by the thrift store and grab a present for Cody's birthday today. He'd promised him he'd be home for dinner; their mom had taken the day off from her second job so she could make Cody's favorite foods: hotdogs and mac and cheese. Carter smiled and shook his head. His stomach growled. *I hope she makes a cake, too.*

Days like today he wished he had a car. He'd get a fancy SUV when he was making the big bucks. He loped up the walkway and took the porch steps in one leap, hoping they hadn't started eating yet. When he opened the door, he was met with the sound of The Dick's too loud voice.

"Ya' little mama's boy crybaby! You're such a spoiled brat! I oughta' smash that cake right in your face."

Carter stomped into the kitchen and stopped inches from The Dick's face. Carter didn't say a word, just crossed his arms at his chest and stood over the drunk loser, glaring. Daring him to make a move. At seventeen, Carter towered over the sorry excuse of a man. He'd outgrown The Dick in both height and muscle mass.

Dick-wad clamped his mouth shut and shrunk into his chair with a scowl, murmuring, "I was just jokin' around."

One look at Cody's red face, jaw clamped tight to stop the tears welling in his eyes, told Carter otherwise. He leaned in close to his stepdad and whispered all Batman-like, "Just keep your mouth shut for the rest of the night."

The drunk's eyes bulged and his throat worked like he was trying to swallow his tongue. Carter knew he wanted to say something but was too big of a sissy. Bullies were all like that, only picking on those who were weaker than them.

Carter knew The Dick still pushed Cody around sometimes, but never when Carter was home. *Coward.*

A vision of a bloody-faced Dick-wad writhing in pain flashed in his mind, and he smiled.

EIGHTEEN

Present Day
Dr. Graves

The television in Dr. Graves' living room was rarely used, but his spirits were still running high from the fishing trip the day before, so he decided to watch *The Princess Bride* for the first time in ages. It felt good to laugh at the purposeful nonsense. He shook his head and smiled at the interaction between Billy Crystal's character and the character's wife.

But that had been Sunday afternoon.

By Sunday night, his thoughts were dragged once again to the serial killer running loose in his beloved community. The doctor's serious demeanor returned. He turned the television off and took his cream soda and Jack Reacher book out to the patio. He couldn't concentrate on the book, so he set it aside and listened to the tree frogs chirp and watched as the lightning bugs flickered on as soon as the sun was set in its cradle for the night.

Dr. Graves stayed out there long past his usual bed time, contemplating how life could bring so many emotions to one man. He smiled to himself as he thought about Kat and the water fight she'd started. His smile faded and his brows creased as his thoughts moved back to the serial killer. What would drive a man to such madness and rage? Mental illness, for sure—no healthy-minded person would commit such heinous acts. But that couldn't be all of it. Dr. Graves knew plenty of people suffering with mental illness who wouldn't so much as swat a fly; good people fighting the good fight to stay as mentally healthy as possible. No, there had to be more to it than that. Most of the cases he'd read about pointed back to a less-than-normal childhood. Something terrible that had happened to set them off on the path of horror.

What was this guy's childhood like? What had happened to him to create the monster? Maybe the blood test results would show something. Dr. Graves was almost certain the last victim would also prove to be an alcoholic like the first one. *That* was the connection.

He slept fitfully and awoke early, heading to work a full hour before usual. Good thing, too. It looked like the coroner had been busy over the weekend. There were three bodies waiting for non-urgent autopsies to determine cause of death.

Dr. Graves was elbow deep into the first one when Kat arrived. She quietly brewed some coffee, then came to stand across from him to assist.

As he sutured up the woman's chest, Kat asked, "Are you okay? You seem rather solemn today."

He attempted a smile, but was pretty sure it looked closer to a grimace. "I'm fine. I just had a rough night, not much sleep."

Kat nodded. "I figured. From the looks of things, you got here quite early." She cocked her head to the side as she clipped the suture for him. "Anything in particular keeping you from sleeping?"

He soaked a handful of four-by-four gauze in a bowl of saline and began wiping the scant amount of blood from the body. "Just trying to make sense of the mind of a serial killer." He shook his head. "What could have caused so much hatred for fellow beings?"

She chewed on the side of her mouth for a few seconds before answering. "I think...you could drive yourself insane trying to figure that out, Dr. Graves. Some things in life just don't make sense no matter how hard you think about them or try to figure them out. The human brain is complex, and when something goes wrong with it... well"—she shrugged—"there's nobody alive or dead that can figure out such a complicated piece of organic machinery."

"I agree," he said. "Unfortunately, that doesn't stop me from obsessing about it." He sighed and zipped the corpse back into the body bag. They cleaned up in silence and prepared the next body for autopsy.

—◊—

TUESDAY STARTED OUT BETTER. He and Kat were able to drink their coffee together in his office before the call from Detective Fitzpatrick destroyed the peaceful morning.

"Graves. Fitzpatrick here."

"*Doctor* Graves, and I know who's calling. What do you have for me?"

"Sorry, Doctor Graves." Pup didn't sound sorry. "Mysterious death at a local club early this morning. Been up since two. I'm following the coroner's van; I'll tell you the deets in person."

"Great." Dr. Graves rolled his shoulders. "I'll see you when you get here."

Without a word, Kat stood and left his office to start getting everything ready.

Dr. Graves sipped his coffee then leaned back in his chair, closing his eyes, only stirring when he heard Kat's voice.

"Hey, Shawn, Pup. I'll go get Dr. Graves."

He met her in the hallway, a small smile playing at his lips as their eyes met. "Here we go again," he quipped.

Kat smiled and nodded.

"Doc!" Fitzpatrick exclaimed. "Long time no see."

"One week is not a long time, detective," Dr. Graves said. "What have you brought us today?"

Pup wagged his head at Shawn, who pulled out his notebook and began his report. "Thirty-two-year-old man, mildly inebriated, was standing at the bar talking to the bartender and a couple of other patrons at around oh-one-hundred to oh-one-thirty. The bartender stated that it appeared the man was chewing on something or playing with something in his mouth. A female he'd been flirting with all night came up behind him and 'goosed him on the butt'—in her own words. The bartender and two other patrons stated that the man slammed his mouth shut. He grabbed the back of his head, then his eyes rolled backwards, he fell to the ground, he arched his neck, and his arms and wrists stiffened before he started convulsing." Detective Davis looked up to make sure Dr. Graves followed along, then continued, "An ambulance was called, but by the time they arrived, the man was not breathing and had no pulse. Attempts to resuscitate were unsuccessful"—he grinned and gestured at the body bag—"as you can plainly see."

Ignoring the detective's grin, Dr. Graves asked, "How soon after the *goosing* did the eye-rolling happen?"

"Within a few seconds of his mouth closing," Fitzpatrick answered.

More to himself than to those in the room, Dr. Graves mumbled, "So, not a case of choking on something."

"It doesn't appear to be that, doctor." Detective Davis shut his notebook and put it back in his pocket.

Dr. Graves nodded. "Okay. If I need any more information from you, I'll call."

Fitzpatrick looked at his partner. "I guess that means we're dismissed."

"Yeah," Davis said. "Let's go get breakfast."

As they prepared the body, Kat asked with a frown, "What do you think happened to him?"

"I'm not sure. Something cerebral from the accounts of his eyes rolling and the convulsions. Maybe he had an aneurysm and it was just bad timing—nothing to do with having something in his mouth or the...uh...*goose*."

After the usual x-rays were obtained, Dr. Graves started to remove the ET tube the paramedics had placed from the deceased's throat. It caught on something on its way out, so he gently wiggled it loose and set it aside. "Shine that light in here." He pried the man's mouth open and carefully inspected his oral cavity. He ran his finger along the man's hard and soft palate. He stopped abruptly and looked up at Kat. "Hand me the curved hemostat."

She handed it to him, a question in her eyes.

"There's something poking out of his palate, I could feel the tip of it." He inserted a mouth retractor and tilted the man's head back. Kat automatically adjusted the lamp, directing the light toward the roof of the man's mouth. Dr. Graves clamped down on the small protrusion and pulled gently. He unclamped the hemostat, shaking his head as he removed the instrument from the mouth. "Whatever it is, it's in there deep. Let's get a CT before I pull it out."

Half an hour later, the CT tech rolled the body back into the morgue. "You'll want to take a look at that right away, Dr. Graves." The tech shook his head. "Something weird in there."

"Thank you, Phillip." Dr. Graves went to his office and logged into the radiology program. He flipped through the CT slices at a quick pace until he got to the base of the brain, where the vertebral arteries lay. He slowed down, flipping back and forth between pictures.

Rushing back into the morgue, he said, "I think I know what happened. Let's see those hemostats again." He tugged on the foreign body with more pressure than he would have thought necessary, then carefully pulled the object from the man's mouth and held it up.

"What is that?" Kat asked, leaning in closer to inspect the thin, two to three-inch object.

Dr. Graves frowned. "A toothpick."

Kat blinked several times, slowly. "So, how did—"

Shaking his head, Dr. Graves said, "Oh, no. You can figure this one out. I'll be in my office. Come tell me when you think you've got it." He set the hemostats and the toothpick on a tray.

She pursed her lips and put her hands on her hips, but he turned and went to his office before she could say anything.

The computer had only just finished booting back up after he signed into the radiology program again when Kat rushed into his office.

The smirk on her face said it all. "He was chewing on the toothpick, probably twisting it around in his mouth. The woman 'goosed' him at just the wrong moment, when the toothpick was pointing up toward the soft palate"—the confidence in her voice faltered a little and she frowned in thought—"the toothpick would have had to be pressed against a tooth or something, though, otherwise, it probably would have just gone through his tongue." She shook her head. "Anyway, the toothpick pierced through his soft palate and into the base of his brain."

Clapping, Dr. Graves smiled and nodded. He turned his monitor toward her. "Exactly right. It was a one in a hundred-million—or more—chance that the toothpick was positioned just right to pierce the basilar artery, here." He pointed at the scan on his screen. "It punctured right where the vertebral arteries come together. I believe his initial reaction, with his eyes rolling back, was due to the blockage caused by the foreign body. His worsening symptoms—loss of consciousness, decerebrate posturing, seizure, and finally, death— were a result of the artery rupturing."

Kat shook her head. "So crazy. Why did his artery rupture with the toothpick still in place? I'm thinking of when you get a nail in your tire and the tire stays inflated until you pull it out."

"Good question." Dr. Graves held his hands up, making a circle the size of a small balloon. "Picture a balloon filled with air, or even water, I guess. If you're really careful, you can put a long needle through one side and out the other without popping the balloon. But if you push all the air, or water, up to where the needle is"—he made a squeezing motion at the bottom of his imaginary balloon—"the added pressure will cause the balloon to pop." He splayed his fingers.

"Ah, makes sense." Kat nodded. "The build-up of blood behind the partial blockage, plus the weakened state of the punctured vessel, caused a catastrophic rupture and bleeding into the base of his brain."

She gestured toward the CT scan on his screen, then tilted her head. "Plus, I imagine his blood pressure spiked initially."

"I imagine so." Dr. Graves turned his monitor back to face him and stood. "Let's finish with the autopsy. We should have the dictation back by tomorrow afternoon, then I'll let you present it to the detectives."

Kat's eyes widened briefly. "Really? You've never let me do that before."

"Well, it's about time I started."

—ʌ—

Eyes wide, Davis pulled the pen lid he'd been chewing out of his mouth and examined it, then shoved it into his pocket. He shook his head. "What are the chances of this happening?"

Kat looked to Dr. Graves for an answer.

He shrugged. "It's the first case I've heard of. So, one in billions, I'd say."

Fitzpatrick slapped the doctor on the shoulder. "Only you, doc." He laughed. "Only you. The medical examiner gods must like messing with you."

Kat rolled her eyes. "So this one gets filed under 'accident.'" She narrowed her eyes and looked at the detectives. "Unless you want to charge the woman with felony *goosing*."

"Or manslaughter by sexual harassment," Dr. Graves added.

Fitzpatrick laughed, and Davis' mouth dropped open before he said, "I didn't know you could joke around, Dr. Graves. I like this side of you."

"Does that mean you don't like the other side of me?" Dr. Graves asked, straight-faced.

"Well, I, uh," the detective stuttered. "Of course I do."

Fitzpatrick slapped him on the back. "Come on, partner. Let's get out of here before you step in it again."

"Have a nice day, detectives," Dr. Graves said.

Walking back to his office, guilt hit him like a punch to the gut. He never joked about the deceased. What had made him do it just now? He ran his hands through his hair. *And I let that ridiculous Detective Fitzpatrick call me "doc."* He shut his office door a little harder than was necessary. Maybe letting himself loosen up around Kat wasn't such a great idea. It appeared to bring out a side of him he hadn't known existed—and wasn't so sure he liked.

NINETEEN

"I love you, buddy." Carter tussled Cody's hair, smiling down at him.

"Love you, too, Carter."

His smile was the best. They both knew Carter would be gone soon. He would turn eighteen in a few months and graduate shortly after that. So he'd made a pact to himself and Cody that he would spend at least one day a week hanging out with him until he set out on his own. Carter always let Cody choose what they did, which was how they ended up at the theater watching the latest Marvel movie and gorging themselves on popcorn soaked in fake butter.

Carter stared down at his brother as he wiped his small oily hand on the pants of his jeans. Cody was the only good thing in his life, and a weight pressed on his chest at the thought of leaving him. In that house. With Dick-wad. Carter had intensified his pleas to their mom, trying to get her to leave. He didn't understand why she stayed. She didn't need that jerk. He contributed absolutely nothing. But she wouldn't go. Carter thought maybe The Dick had threatened to hurt her or Cody if she did.

Carter sighed and looked back at the big screen. He loved his mother, but her weakness disgusted him.

Cody jumped in his seat and covered his eyes as the villain threw a car at one of the heroes. Carter put a hand on his brother's shoulder and laughed. Yeah, Cody was the best.

And then it hit him—why not take him with him?

Their mom, too, if she'd come, but Cody for sure.

Mrs. Crowther, his school counselor, had helped him secure enough scholarship and grant money to pay for school and housing. Carter's smile widened, and that weight, the one on his chest, it lifted. That was the new plan. Him and Cody, bachelor-ing it up in a cheap apartment near the college.

Carter rested his arm across his brother's shoulders, and Cody leaned into him, his eyes glued to the action on the screen.

TWENTY

Present Day
Dr. Graves

The light was on in Kat's office. She must have come in a little early. Dr. Graves slipped quietly into his office without walking the few extra steps to hers to say "good morning" as he usually did. She'd texted him a couple of times over the weekend, worried about him, she'd said, and he'd answered—because ignoring her would be rude—but his answers had been short and dismissive. And now he felt horrible about it. And a little ashamed. He'd thought that getting back to his normal weekend routine was what he needed, but his normal routine didn't feel like it used to.

He *liked* spending time with Kat.

A soft knock at his door made him straighten his posture and pretend to concentrate on his computer monitor, which hadn't yet been turned on.

"Good morning, Dr. Graves," Kat said as she opened the door a crack and peeked in. "Coffee?" In her hand, she held a cup from his favorite little coffee shop around the corner. So much better than what they brewed in the ancient pot here at the office.

The smell wafted toward him, and he breathed deeply, closing his eyes on a long blink. "Yes. Thank you very much, Kat."

She set the cup on his desk, then turned to go. When she reached the door, she looked back over her shoulder. "Oh, and the lab report is up."

There was no need to tell him which lab report; he'd been

waiting two weeks for the labs of the last victim of the serial killer. He nodded to her and she slipped out, closing his door behind her. He sipped his coffee while he waited for his computer to boot up. He should probably apologize to Kat. Maybe invite her to lunch to make up for it.

Dr. Graves leaned forward to type in his credentials to gain access to the lab results. He typed in the victim's number and held his breath. When he read the results for the PEth, the main test he was interested in, he whispered, "I knew it."

He instinctively yelled, "Kat!" Then he winced, remembering how he'd avoided her this weekend.

Her shoes squeaked on the hallway tile before she entered his office. "Everything okay?"

"Yeah." He ducked his head. He owed her an apology, but it would have to come later. Looking back up at her, he was relieved to see her smile. "The lab results showed exactly what I thought they would. Victim number two was a heavy drinker, too. I mean, we knew that from how his liver looked, but the PEth numbers came in at greater than 200ng/ml."

"What does that mean?" Kat asked.

"It means that this man was a chronic alcoholic, just like our first victim."

Kat nodded and sat in the chair across from his desk. "So, we can add that to the list of victims' traits the killer goes for—chronic alcoholism, middle aged, tall, big build, male. Anything else?"

"No, I think that's it. Both victims disappeared from bars."

"And not high-end clubs; they were pretty much dive bars," Kat added.

"Yeah. I'm going to call Chief Billings. Anything else you can think of that might help in their investigation?"

"Nothing I can think of at the moment." She stood and turned toward the door.

"Will you do me a favor?" Dr. Graves asked. "Will you get me a list of 'dive bars,' as you put it, in the area?"

She turned her head slowly to look at him with a deep crease in her forehead and narrowed eyes. "Why?"

"I just want to map them out. See if I can narrow down where his next victim might come from." He wasn't being completely honest. A crazy idea had begun to form over the long weekend.

"Okay. Yeah, I can do that."

"Thank you." Dr. Graves turned his attention back to his computer screen to look at the other lab results. Kat left the office, shutting the door behind her.

He picked up the phone and dialed Tracey's number. She picked up on the third ring.

"Chief Billings."

"Hi, Tracey," Dr. Graves said. "I have the lab results for our second victim."

"Well?"

"This victim was, as expected, a chronic alcoholic like the last one. I think that's important to the killer—he's going after men who drink a lot. Also, the paralytic he used was a different kind than last time. This time we picked up traces of rocuronium in the blood and liver."

"What do you think that means? What's the difference?"

"The main difference is in the length of time it takes to work and its duration. Succinylcholine has a quicker onset of action and has a duration of only around five minutes. Rocuronium can take a couple of minutes to work, but it lasts anywhere from thirty to ninety minutes."

Tracey tapped her fingernails on her desk, the sound slightly muted through the receiver. "Why do you think he switched?"

"Well, my guess is he just uses what he can get his hands on. But maybe it's more than that, maybe he wanted a longer amount of time to torture? I don't know."

Tracey hummed softly, something she often did when thinking. "Maybe it's time to re-canvas the surgical centers and hospitals. I really don't know where else to go from here."

"I have some ideas. Kat is working on something for me, I'll give you a call when I have a more formal proposal for you."

"I appreciate it, Dean. You're the smartest man I know, and I'm glad you're invested in finding this creep."

"Wait," Dr. Graves said with a grin, "are you saying I'm smarter than Detective Fitzpatrick?"

"Ha!" Tracey slapped her desk. "My Boston Terrier is smarter than Pup." Then, in a lower voice she added, "Don't tell him I said that."

"Your secret is safe with me."

"I'm liking this new, more relaxed version of you, Dr. Graves." Tracey laughed.

He frowned and mumbled, "You're the second person in less than a week who has said that."

"Well, that's a good thing, isn't it? That you're loosening up a little?"

"I haven't quite decided if it's a good or a bad thing yet."

"I vote for good," Tracey said. "I gotta go. Give me a call when you finish up that proposal."

The phone clicked in his ear before he could answer her.

He spent the next couple of hours thinking, planning, and scratching notes onto a yellow legal pad.

Dr. Graves had just set his mechanical pencil down, his face tightened around a frown, when Kat tapped on his door, then let herself in.

"Here's your list of bars. The first section lists bars close to where the victims were found, the second section lists bars in town, and the third section is farther out—on the outskirts of Augusta."

Reaching to take the paper from her, he smiled thinly. "Thank you."

"You're welcome."

Dr. Graves looked at his watch then back up at Kat.

At the exact same time as he said, "Would you like to go get lunch?", she said, "Wanna go get something to eat?"

As they laughed, Dr. Graves locked his computer screen and stood. "Where would you like to go?"

"The pizza place?" Kat tilted her head.

Dr. Graves nodded. The sliding doors opened and they stepped through. Kat pushed the button to summon the elevator, and they stood in silence for a moment as they waited.

The elevator seemed to be stopping at every floor before descending to their basement digs. Kat looked up at him. "Are you okay?"

"I—I think so," he answered. "Why do you ask?" Was it that obvious something was bothering him?

She quirked an eyebrow in his direction. "You 'think so'?"

"Well, I mean..." *How to explain?* "I—"

The elevator doors opened and they stepped inside.

Dr. Graves took a deep breath and turned to face her. "I owe you an apology, Kat." He ran a hand through his disheveled hair. "Since I've been...hanging out...with you...some...I, well...I seem to be changing, a little."

Kat nodded.

He looked up at the ceiling. The elevator stopped on the main floor and they walked silently to the exit and outside, where Dr. Graves continued his disordered explanation. "Anyway, I like some of the changes. Most of the changes. I'm a bit more jovial, which is good, except when it isn't."

"For example?" Kat asked, taking one and a half steps for his every one.

Heat flushed up from his neck. He pulled at his collar and considered unbuttoning the top button. Shame almost kept him from declaring his confession. He stopped and looked down and waited for her to stop beside him. "The other day, I, uh, I made a *joke* about one of the deceased."

Kat was quiet for several erratic beats of his heart. "You're talking about the 'manslaughter' comment?" she finally said.

His head dropped even lower; his chin touched his chest. "Yes."

Positioning herself in front of him, she put a warm hand on his arm and waited until he looked at her. "Dean, it's okay to find humor in tragedy, you know. Sometimes that's the best way to cope with the difficult things you face in your job."

He shook his head and opened his mouth to respond, but Kat put her finger to his lips to silence him.

"You," she said with authority, "are the most respectful man I've ever met. Your respect and gentleness toward the dead is my favorite thing about you. I'm sorry if my...irreverence, the other day led to the minuscule lapse in your very high standards. I will strive to do better."

Dr. Graves licked his lips where her finger had pressed. He looked away from her. "No, no, I don't want you to change a thing about yourself. This is on me. I either need to find a way to control my impulses better with the new lightness in my heart, or"—his voice dropped to a near whisper—"go back to the way things were."

Her eyes welled with tears, followed by a flash of anger, before she turned her back to him. "Well," she said, "I see. I suddenly don't feel like eating. I'm going to go back to the office and get some filing done." She walked back toward the examiner's office at a brisk pace, leaving Dr. Graves wondering what he'd just done.

TWENTY ONE

Ten Years Ago
Carter, age 18

"Congratulations, Carter." Mr. Thompson, the math teacher, clapped a hand on his back.

"Thanks, Mr. Thompson. I'd better get inside; it looks like they're getting us all lined up."

The teacher smiled and nodded.

Carter hurried through the backstage door to the auditorium, his heart beating fast to match his excitement. This was it. Graduation. He'd already packed up his meager belongings and they waited in his bedroom in the home he would no longer call his after tonight. He thought about Cody. And their mom. She refused to leave Dick-wad, but after many discussions, only a few of which Carter raised his voice, she consented to let Cody go with him to college.

The clincher took place just a couple of weeks ago, when Carter had been at an early graduation party and The Dick had taken full advantage of his absence. Their mom had come home from the late shift to find Cody barricaded in his bedroom while The Dick destroyed the living room. Cody's left eye was swollen shut, and she knew that once Carter left, the abuse would ramp up again.

So, Cody's stuff was packed and waiting at the house, too. They'd move into their bachelor pad the next day. A two-hour bus ride away from this nightmare.

Carter pulled his phone out of his pocket. He'd missed a call from his mom. He listened to the voicemail telling him they were running late, then he deleted it and shoved it back in his pocket beneath the gown before finding his place in line outside the auditorium.

—⋀—

THE GRADUATION CEREMONY was almost over. Carter searched the crowd for the hundredth time, but he still couldn't find Cody or his mom. There were a ton of people there, though, so it wasn't that weird that he couldn't see them, although he'd been surprised they hadn't yelled out and clapped for him when his name was read. Cody had been practicing his *whoop* for a week now. Maybe he'd chickened out when he saw how many people were there.

The graduates stood and moved their tassels from one side of the cardboard hat to the other, then, with shouts of joy, they all threw their caps in the air. As the graduates and spectators filed out of the auditorium to the lawn just outside, the principal stepped into the crowd and grabbed Carter by the arm, his mouth fixed in a grim line.

Carter's heart skipped a beat.

The principal led him back inside to a deserted classroom down the hall, where two police officers waited.

"Carter Ridge?" one of them asked.

Carter nodded, his throat too constricted to speak.

"There's been an accident." The officer looked to the principal, swallowed, then looked back at Carter. "There's no easy way to say this. Your mom and brother were killed in a car accident. Your stepdad was taken to the hospital, but appears to be fine."

"No." Carter shook his head.

The principal put a hand on his shoulder.

"No. It can't...it can't be true." He looked at the officers. "I want to see them."

The officer who'd spoken looked down. "I'm afraid that's not possible right now. It's a criminal case, so their bodies were taken to the M.E." He looked up, into Carter's eyes. "I don't think you want to see them either way, son. It...it was a mess."

"Criminal case?" Red, hot flames shot up Carter's neck and face.

"Yeah...um." The officer looked at his partner, then back at Carter. "Your...um, stepdad was driving, and he...he was really drunk."

Blinding rage seared his vision. His heart hammered with a dangerous mixture of hatred and fury for that putrid maggot drunk, and crippling grief for Cody and his mom.

"I'll kill that bastard," Carter whispered through clenched teeth. He wrenched away from the principal's soft grip on his shoulder. "I'll kill him!" he shouted.

One of the officers blocked his exit, hands up chest high, palms out in a placating manner. "He's on his way to jail now. He'll get his punishment."

Carter breathed in and out too fast, shakily.

My baby brother. My mom. Dead.

Because of him.

And he walked away.

He nodded to the officers, but inside, a picture started to form of what he'd do to Richard when he got the chance.

I will kill him.

Happy graduation to me.

TWENTY TWO

PRESENT DAY
Dr. Graves

The Barking Dog Bar. Dr. Graves squinted as he surveyed the dark surroundings. The country music playing over the speakers made it impossible for him to eavesdrop on any conversations more than a few feet away, even though the patrons were practically yelling to be heard over the din. He took another sip of his water, no ice. The bartender had not been happy with the order, mumbling something about needing to start a minimum drink requirement, so Dr. Graves ordered some nachos to appease him.

A plate of stale nachos, several glasses of water, and three and a half hours later, Dr. Graves had seen a few men that might fit the victim profile of the killer, but hadn't seen anyone that seemed to be lurking or watching them closely. And it was now nearing midnight. Dr. Graves yawned. Six A.M. was going to come early.

He pulled the list of bars Kat had made for him out of his pocket and used the light from his cell phone to look at it. He'd go to Lucky Seven tomorrow.

He'd suggested to Chief Billings that she have officers staked out at several of the bars each night, but she just laughed and said, "Yeah, right. Have you seen my budget? Have you seen our call stats?" He hadn't mentioned to her that he would just do it himself. She'd have just tried to talk him out of it.

He tipped the bartender and made his way to the door. He'd

been a little surprised at the number of people there on a Monday night. It wasn't even football season.

On the drive home, his mind drifted to Kat. She'd stayed tucked away in her office for the rest of the day; the only words she spoke to him after their failed lunch date were "See you tomorrow," as she walked past his office on her way out.

He'd really screwed up. Maybe it was for the best.

The pit in his stomach didn't agree.

As the alarm blared the next morning, he groaned. He felt like he'd just fallen asleep. He stopped and got coffee for him and Kat, leaving hers next to her keyboard, as she hadn't arrived yet. He sat at his desk, pulled the list out, and crossed The Barking Dog off of it. The bar hadn't really started to get busy until after eight last night, so maybe he could take a nap before heading to the Lucky Seven tonight.

They had two routine unwitnessed death autopsies on the schedule. Kat only spoke to him when necessary, only about work, and mostly with one-word answers. Her hand didn't *accidentally* brush against his when handing him instruments—which, he realized mid-day, meant that the other times hadn't been accidental at all. He studied her as she prepared some tissue samples for the lab. She didn't seem to be angry. Was the look in her eyes when she half-smiled at him one of hurt? He sighed. Things had been so much simpler before he noticed his attraction to her.

Toward the end of the day, Dr. Graves caved to his exhaustion and cradled his head in his arms on his desk. He looked up at a knock on his open door.

"Are you okay?" Kat asked, her brow furrowed with worry.

He cleared his throat. "Yes. I'm just tired."

"Well"—she straightened her purse strap across her shoulder—"do you need anything else before I leave?"

"No. Have a good evening. I'll see you tomorrow." He attempted to smile but was afraid it came off more like a grimace.

Kat nodded and turned toward the door, hesitating before stepping through. "I..." She shook her head slightly, then continued out of the office.

Dr. Graves laid his head back down, deciding to just catch a few winks at his desk instead of going home—afraid that if he did, he'd have a hard time going back out.

Something bumped into the wall next to his office, the noise jerking him awake. He looked at his watch, rubbed his eyes, and looked again. He'd been asleep at his desk for a couple of hours, and his neck and shoulder muscles screamed in discomfort. He stood and stretched, then swiped his hands over his face. Stuffing his notebook and pencil into his jacket pocket, he glanced around his office with the feeling he was forgetting something. His keys jingled as he patted his pants pocket.

Shaking his head, Dr. Graves stepped into the hallway, locked his door, then shut it. He nodded to the housekeeper, whose cart bumping into the wall had been the impetus for his awakening. The housekeeper nodded back then reached into his breast pocket for his buzzing phone.

Dr. Graves stopped in his tracks and slapped at his pockets. He'd forgotten his phone.

After he retrieved it and other necessary items, he used his navigation system to drive to the Lucky Seven.

Once there, he positioned himself at the end of the bar where he could see most of the other patrons. He ordered his water, no ice, and at a derisive look from the bartender, ordered some chicken strips. Then he settled in for a long evening.

Around ten, Dr. Graves focused on a man sitting on a stool mid-bar, about five seats away from him. All of the employees seemed to know him by name. The bartender set a drink before him without an order being placed. *This guy comes here a lot.*

The guy wasn't exactly the right stature, but Dr. Graves watched him down drink after drink, getting louder and more obnoxious with each passing moment. The doctor watched the other patrons to see if anyone else was paying particular attention to the man. As it neared midnight, he still hadn't seen any suspicious lurkers. He decided to call it a night, but the thought occurred to him that he should take some pictures of the drunkard and those near him. It could be useful if the man came up missing—or dead.

Dr. Graves snapped three pictures and turned on his stool to get one more of the diminishing crowd. A short but stout man stepped in front of his camera phone, grabbed it, threw it to the cement floor, and stomped it with his well-worn work boot.

Dr. Graves stood, mouth agape, looking from his shattered phone to the aggressor who'd smashed it. Anger borne of fatigue and worry —and knowing there was a monstrous killer on the loose—flared in his chest. He pushed the guy and growled, "What the hell?"

Stumbling backward, the guy said, "No one takes pictures of my girlfriend!"

"I wasn't—"

A meaty fist slammed into Dr. Graves' temple, twisting him so his upper body sprawled onto the bar. He pushed off the countertop, shaking the wooziness from his head. Drops of blood splashed onto the bar and into his eyes. He took a deep breath before straightening up and turning to face the man, vacillating between whether to tackle the jerk to the ground or try to reason with him. Dr. Graves rolled his shoulders, high school wrestling champion moves flitting across his thoughts. Two burly bouncers grabbed the guy by the arms and drug him toward the exit as he yelled profanities.

One of the waitresses handed Dr. Graves a pile of napkins. "Are you okay?"

He pressed the napkins to his left brow and nodded, then took a step away from the bar, intent on leaving. He swayed a little and the waitress grabbed onto his arm.

She guided him back to the barstool. "You should sit down for a bit." She took the napkins from his hand and dipped them in his water. "Here, let me clean that up for you." She leaned in, pressing her body against his arm, breathing into his ear.

Dr. Graves winced as she cleaned the blood around his eye.

"Sorry," she whispered. "You're gonna need some stitches. It's a pity that such a handsome face will have a scar."

"He must have been wearing a ring," Dr. Graves said absently. He glanced at the waitress, and she smiled and licked her lips. *Wait. Is she flirting with me?* He smiled back but leaned away from her a few inches. He took her handful of napkins and lowered it from his head. "Thank you for your help. I'd better go see about those stitches."

She handed him a clean napkin, and he held it to his still bleeding head. "See you later," she said. "I hope."

He picked up what remained of his phone, leaving the small pieces of glass behind, and dropped it in his shirt pocket.

Out in his car, he examined the wound. It began about a half inch above his left eyebrow, jutting down to slice clean through the eyebrow itself. It gaped open. The flirty waitress was right, it needed sutures. He sighed, looking at the clock. Twelve-thirty. He started his car and drove to the morgue.

—⋀—

A LIGHT RAP on his door jerked the doctor awake. He sat up too quickly and pain shot through his head. He looked at his surroundings through squinting eyes, and memories of the events that took place the prior evening rushed in. He winced. He'd fallen asleep on the small, two-person couch in his office after stitching himself up. His legs were numb at the knees from hanging over the edge, and every muscle from his neck down whimpered with stiffness.

"Dr. Graves?" Kat said through the door. "Are you in there?"

He cleared the morning phlegm from his throat. "Yes, um, give me just a minute."

"Is everything okay?"

His heart skipped at the worried note in her voice. "Yes. Everything's fine." He stood and looked down at his wrinkled clothes —the same ones he'd worn yesterday. He grabbed his lab coat from its hook on the wall and slipped it on, then ran his fingers through his hair. *Is the bed-head look still in?*

Flipping the light on, he unlocked and opened the door to his office. He didn't remember locking it.

Kat gasped. "What happened to you?" She squeezed past him and hurried to his desk to set two coffees down before returning to stand in front of him. She raised up on her toes and gently pushed his chin to the side, examining the left side of his face. She pursed her lips, a scowl racing across her forehead. "You look like you've been in a fight."

He looked longingly at the coffee, the odor wafting through the room. He thought about lying, saying he'd run into a door or something. But lying wasn't his thing and, besides, Kat worked in forensics; she'd know.

"Well, it wasn't much of a fight on my end." His attempt at humor fell flat.

"Are you going to tell me what happened?" She stared him straight in the eyes.

Sighing, Dr. Graves shifted his gaze away from hers, staring at the wall over her shoulder. He gestured to his desk. "Let's have a seat. I need that coffee you brought me." He looked at her then. "And, thank you for bringing it."

Kat's face softened just enough for him to notice, and he pulled his lips into an exhausted smile before going to his desk and sitting down. He took a long sip of the hot coffee and closed his eyes as it flowed to his stomach. When he opened his eyes, Kat stared at him with her arms crossed. "Okay," he said. "I went to a bar last night, just to scope it out, and a guy hit me because he thought I was taking a picture of his girlfriend."

"You—you went to a *bar*?" She leaned forward and put her hands on his desk, her knuckles white with the pressure she put on them.

"Does this have something to do with that list you asked me to make? The one you were going to use to 'map out' the area?"

He couldn't look her in the eyes. "Well, I, uh—" Why did it feel like he was in the principal's office? He shook his head, sending another jolt of pain through his brain. He really didn't *have* to answer. He glanced up at her, then back down at his hands. "Yes. I went to one of the bars on your list. Two, actually; I went to one on Monday night also."

With a slow shake of her head, lips pursed, she took a breath through her nose before speaking. "Why?" Her voice was a low growl.

Frustration leaked through his exhaustion. "Dammit, Kat, we have to catch this guy!" He ran his hands through his hair, wincing at the pull on his eyebrow sutures. "I don't want to wade through another of his psychotic murder scenes. See another human tortured and flayed. Have a thousand thoughts swirling around in my head night and day about the incomprehensible suffering he creates." He wiped angrily at a tear that fled down his face without his permission.

Kat matched his frustration with her own. "Except that isn't your job! Why can't you just let the police do their job and you stay safely here, doing yours?" Her voice softened at the end and she looked away.

"I tried going that avenue, Kat. Chief Billings doesn't have the manpower or the budget to scope out the bars. And this"—he gestured to his face, and she finally looked his way again—"is in no way related to our killer. It's just something that happens in bars."

She let out a scornful laugh. "Only on TV, De...Dr. Graves. I go to bars and clubs all the time, and I've never seen a fist fight. What you're doing is dangerous—"

"Why do you care?" The irritation returned to his voice even though his fuzzy mind tried to prevent it. "It's really not something you need to concern yourself with." He winced at the coldness of his own words. Maybe his head injury was causing him to behave so unlike himself. He shook his head and grimaced at the pain, opening his mouth to apologize—

"You're right, Dr. Graves." She stood. "Except for one thing—I gave you that list and that makes me complicit in your current and future injuries—or death." She spun around and stomped to her office.

Dr. Graves dropped his head into his folded arms on his desk.

TWENTY THREE

PRESENT DAY
Carter, age 28

Tonight was the night. Signaling the waitress, Carter ordered another round of drinks for his two tablemates. He ground his teeth, trying to keep up the smile as he wished the other guy would leave. Go home to his stupid dog he wouldn't shut-up about.

Carter tilted his head back and laughed at *the drunk's* attempts to be funny, feeding him more and more alcohol until his speech came out in incomprehensible slurs. Until he could barely keep his eyes open. Carter needed to figure out a way to get him to the 4Runner while he could still walk. He glanced up to scout a trail to the door, and the guy sitting at the table across from them looked right at him. Stared at him.

What's his deal? Carter's stomach twisted. *He knows. Somehow.*

The server-chick stepped between Carter and the staring man, and Carter shook his head, laughing at his newfound paranoia. *He can't know. I can't be caught. I have honor and justice on my side. I'm a superhero. They'll never catch me.*

The staring man stood and walked to the exit, fumbling for something in his pocket. He didn't look back.

Yeah, he has no idea. Carter straightened his baseball cap and turned his attention back to *the drunk,* his confidence fully restored. The third-wheel excused himself to the bathroom, and Carter knew fate was on his side.

He smiled. "Come on, buddy. Let me give you a ride home."

TWENTY FOUR

Present Day
Dr. Graves

Having a concussion and still going to work each day was... inconvenient, often painful, and probably not the best idea. But, the coolness with which his best and closest coworker and friend —maybe *former* friend, though he sincerely hoped not—regarded Dr. Graves was pure torture. He wanted to make things right with Kat, but his head still buzzed and his thoughts were fuzzy, and he was still prone to bouts of irritability with which he did not under any circumstances want to subject her to again.

So they worked side-by-side in silence while performing autopsies, and each stayed in their own office otherwise.

He'd taken a couple of nights off from his bar surveillance, going home as soon as possible after work, taking ibuprofen, and going to bed. But tonight, he planned to resume. He looked at his watch. Six-thirty. Kat had long since left the morgue, and the housekeeper had come and gone an hour ago.

It was Friday night, so the bar should have an earlier crowd.

Dr. Graves changed into jeans and a t-shirt, hoping to more easily be lost in the crowd. As he pushed his wallet into his back pocket, he wished he'd had the energy to replace his phone. Part of him hadn't wanted to, though, because it kept him from texting something to Kat that he wouldn't be able to take back. He wasn't worried about sending her a rude message. More the opposite. Ever since their... mental parting of the ways, he'd become more and more aware of how much he enjoyed her company. He missed their workplace banter and the easy way with which Kat interacted with him—not an easy feat from his past experiences.

Grabbing his keys up off his desk, he left, locking his office behind him. He lamented the loss of his phone and photo taking abilities all the way out to his car. He programmed "Snake Eyes Bar and Grille" into his car's navigation system and headed out.

There really wasn't a good spot from which to observe the crowd at the Snake Eyes; there were too many high-backed booths and half-walls in the way. Dr. Graves ordered a beer, having learned his lesson about ordering water in a place like this. His intention was to wander around, holding the bottle in his hand as if he intended to drink it, whilst looking for any patrons that might fit his profile of the victims. He'd never liked beer—or any form of alcoholic beverage, for that matter—yet he had a sudden craving to actually drink the cold one he held in his hand. Even as the logical part of his brain warned him that alcohol combined with a recent head injury was not a good idea, he took a sip. The cold brew slid down his throat and actually didn't taste as awful as he remembered from the one time in college he'd been coerced into trying it. His face only twisted up into a slight grimace instead of the Tasmanian Devil-like face he'd made way back when.

Dr. Graves wandered and sipped, determined to make the one beer last throughout the night. By nine o'clock, the bottle was nearly empty and his feet ached. He slid into a newly evacuated booth across from a trio of obnoxiously loud men. After listening in on the conversation and sneaking glances at them, he realized it was really only two of the men who were being rowdy, the third man appeared to be just listening in, injecting the occasional question or comment, and buying drinks for his two inebriated friends.

A waitress approached his table, blocking his view of the men. "Can I get you another drink?"

Dr. Graves glanced down at the now empty bottle still grasped in his hand on the table, then squinted up at her. "No. No, thank you."

The waitress's smile faltered.

He looked around at the crowded bar; more people shuffled through the front doors. "I'll be leaving soon," he said with a smile.

"Okay, let me know if you need anything else before you go."

It was after ten, and the music cranked up, the crowd noise increasing in response. Dr. Graves' head pounded with the bass and the yells and the clink of glassware. Any and all energy fled his body, leaving him beyond exhausted. It took all his concentration to pull his wallet out and flip a twenty-dollar bill onto the table to make up for his guilt at taking up space and only buying one beer.

He stood and cast another glance at the table across from him, a hazy thought flickering in the back of his mind. He reached for the pocket that usually contained his phone and scowled when he remembered it wasn't there. He would have liked to take a picture to study when his brain cleared a little. He only realized he'd been staring at the sober man of the trio when the guy met his eyes with a narrow, fixed gaze beneath the brim of a baseball cap. A glint of something odd there, in those eyes...

The spell was broken as the waitress stepped between them, facing Dr. Graves. "Thank you for the gracious tip. I didn't mean to rush you out of here." She touched his arm and smiled.

He barely registered her touch, the pounding in his head increasing by the second. What had he been thinking a moment ago? He shrugged her hand away and ambled toward the exit, fumbling for his keys.

—∿—

ON SATURDAY DR. GRAVES tried to finish a painting out on his deck, but only lasted about ten minutes before settling into a chair to sip at his cream soda. Winston, the neighbor's dog, trotted over and laid his head on the doctor's lap. He didn't even try to pretend he was annoyed by this, just stroked the dog's head, contemplating how animals seemed to sense things humans couldn't. Like how Dr. Graves was in no mood or physical state to play fetch today.

After about a half-hour of dog therapy, Winston's owner called him home, and Dr. Graves went inside to prepare for that night's foray into the world of amateur surveillance. *No alcoholic beverages tonight*, he promised himself.

—⋀—

SUNDAY HAD TRULY BEEN a day of rest. After not seeing anything of interest at the bar on Saturday night, Dr. Graves had spent all of Sunday resting, trying to coax his brain back into shape. Something still nagged at him about his time spent at the Snake Eye on Friday, but he couldn't pull it to the forefront of his mind.

He reached for his sunglasses as the sun peeked over the horizon on his drive in to work. He needed to make things right with Kat. That much had slunk its way into his thoughts as he lay with lights off and eyes closed yesterday. His stomach lurched at the thought.

He pulled into the parking lot, his was the first car there. He took a deep breath before turning it off and opening the door. He hoped it was a slow day at the morgue today.

A pile of dictation awaited him in a manila envelope marked as "CONFIDENTIAL" in the basket attached to his door. He always thoroughly proofread his dictation before signing, striking out and fixing the inevitable errors he found. Sitting at his desk he vacillated about whether to keep the lights low and strain to see the print, or turn the lights up and risk getting another headache. He decided not to decide and typed out an email to Chief Billings instead.

A quiet tap on his door drew his attention away from the Monday morning conundrum. He looked up and cleared his throat. "Come in."

"Dr. Graves," Kat said, "can we talk?"

Warning sirens blared to life in his chest, choking off his next breath. What if she was quitting? Just the idea of it scared him…and it scared him that it scared him. He ran his hands through his hair and cleared his throat again. "Okay."

She sat across from him and looked him in the eye. "I owe you an apology."

He released his held breath and cocked his head to the side. "*You* owe *me* an apology? Kat—"

"Let me finish, please." She smiled softly. "I'm sorry I let my worry for you come out in a way that sounded confrontational." She raised her eyes to the ceiling. "In a way that *was* confrontational. You were right; it's none of my concern what you do with your free time, and I shouldn't have let it affect our working relationship. I care about your safety, but I will try to keep those opinions to myself from now on."

"Kat." He so badly wanted to reach across the desk and take her hand. "Thank you for that. But you do not need to apologize to me. I was the one that was out of line. I want to blame getting knocked in the head for my irritable state, but that is no excuse for acting the way I did. Please forgive me. You are invaluable to me." He let the rest of that thought fade into the surrounding atmosphere.

"Well..." She tried to smile again, but it looked sad. "Let's just chalk it up to bad behavior on both sides and move on." She looked at his eyebrow. "We should probably remove those sutures today; it's been six days."

"I would appreciate your assistance with that. Why don't you go get started on your morning routine, and you can take them out when you're ready?" He needed a minute to calm his erratic heart and shaking hands. She wasn't leaving him—the *M.E.'s* office. She wasn't leaving the M.E.'s office.

As soon as he heard her office door open and the lights flipped on, he dropped his head into his hands, allowing himself a couple of minutes to analyze his reaction. Was it all because she was such a hard-working and thorough assistant? Could he fool himself into believing that was the cause of his great distress at the thought of... losing her? And what did he mean by "losing her"? His mind kept trying to convince his heart that he just meant losing her as an employee.

"Gah!" He tangled his hands in his hair. All this uncharted emotion mess would have to wait. He had a serial killer to catch.

Dr. Graves had just finished filing the last dictated report when he turned to find Kat at his door, suture removal kit in hand. "Are you ready?" she asked.

He nodded. "Where would you like me?"

She raised an eyebrow, a little bit of her old self rising to the surface. "I think it will work if you just sit in your chair and tilt your head back on top of the backrest."

As she worked carefully to pull up and then snip each suture, her reading glasses slipping down the bridge of her nose, Dr. Graves studied her with one open eye. He clenched his fists on the arms of his chair as her touch caused his skin to burn with warmth.

"Sorry," she stopped and looked at him. "Did that one hurt?"

"Umm, no. Just, thinking about something."

She repositioned his face to the ceiling, again causing the warmth to radiate from her hands to his skin and straight to his heart.

"So," she said, wrinkling her brow as she worked, "are you going bar-gazing tonight?"

He chuckled. "Yes. I took yesterday off so I really need to go tonight."

She nodded and placed another removed suture on the gauze sitting on his desk. "Have you replaced your phone yet?"

"Not yet."

She pulled up on another stitch and slid the scissors under it. "Maybe I should come with you tonight. I'll bring my phone."

He wanted to say no, that it was too dangerous. But that would be too disingenuous after he'd insisted he wasn't in any danger. "You don't have to do that. I usually stay rather late."

"It's not like I can sleep anyway."

He winced as she pulled just a little too hard on the next stitch. He realized he couldn't stop her from going any more than she could stop him. They were both adults. "Okay. I'd like the company, actually. People always look at me weird when I'm sitting there by myself drinking water. And strange women always seem to want to remedy that by sliding next to me and talking. It's distracting."

Kat laughed. "If any other man said that I'd think he was bragging. But not you."

His thoughts flew back in time, remembering when she'd called him out on the fact that he couldn't tell when a woman was flirting with him.

Placing the last of the six sutures on the gauze, Kat studied the healing wound. "It looks pretty good. You'll have a scar right through your eyebrow, though."

"Just like Jason Momoa," he mumbled.

Kat raised an eyebrow and stood back, examining his face. "Hmm. Yeah. It's not fair how things like this add to the appeal of a man but not a woman."

He had no idea what she meant. How could a scar be appealing?

"So..." She swiped the gauze into the waste basket. "What time and what bar?" Her voice changed back to the muted version when she said, "I'll, um, meet you there."

The elevator dinged, announcing its arrival on their floor. The thin walls down there used to annoy Dr. Graves, but he was used to it now, mostly. It gave him a moment to swallow down an offer to give Kat a ride. She didn't want to ride with him, he was sure. "The Rabble Rousers is the name of the bar, and I plan on being there around eight o'clock." Of course, he would arrive early so Kat wouldn't be there by herself.

A uniformed police officer stepped to his door and cleared his throat.

"Come in," Dr. Graves said.

"Chief sent these reports over. Where do you want them?"

Dr. Graves gestured to the corner of his desk. "Just set them there, I'll look through them tomorrow."

—⋀—

THEY SAT in silence at the bar, water with no ice for him, and a margarita for her. It was near midnight, and Dr. Graves was ready to call it a night. Kat hadn't even had to use her phone, as there were no men there that fit the victims' profile. That wasn't why Dr. Graves was feeling so morose, though. He longed for the easy connection he and Kat used to have, exasperated that he'd ruined it, and clueless as to how to bring about its return.

He glanced at her as she stared blankly at the pictures above the bar. Then he glanced past her and noticed a couple of younger guys looking at her, smiling, trying to catch her eye.

With a scowl, Dr. Graves turned away from them and cleared his throat. "Well, I guess we should call it a night. We aren't apt to see any new faces this late on a Monday night."

As he scooted off the stool, the two men stood and moved as if to take his place beside Kat. Reflexively, he rested his hand on her arm near the elbow, resisting the pull to "help" her up. In a low voice he said, "Please allow me to walk you to your car."

"Okay, Dr. Graves. Let's blow this joint." Kat leaned in to take one last sip of her drink.

"Aren't you supposed to *inhale* joints?" he asked, having no idea how his brain let that slip out his mouth.

Kat spewed her margarita all over the top of the bar and cough-laughed as she turned to face him. The old Kat appeared in her eyes in the form of a mischievous sparkle, and she wiped her mouth with the back of her hand. "Well, Dr. Graves, you must be tired if you're cracking THC jokes."

Her use of the abbreviation for the chemical compound that makes up the majority of the psychoactive part of marijuana made it even funnier to him. He laughed as he helped her off the stool, the pressure that had been squeezing his chest since last week eased—and floated entirely away when she took his arm as they left the bar.

At her car he said, "Thank you for your company tonight."

"I'm afraid I wasn't very good company. Just thinking about the killer, that he could be sitting just down the bar or at a table behind us..." She shuddered.

He bowed his head and whispered, "Yeah. I know."

—◦—

His head hit the pillow at twelve-thirty-nine.

He jerked awake at five-twenty-three, to the sound of his house phone ringing.

TWENTY FIVE

PRESENT DAY
Dr. Graves

D r. Graves slammed his fist on the steering wheel, veering to the side of the highway and onto the rumble strips. He took in a deep breath as he corrected his course then let it out slowly. Another victim. This one at an abandoned elementary school. He tightened his grip until it hurt.

It wasn't hard to find where to enter the building. A red and blue dance of lights led the way, followed by yellow tape being strewn around the entrance by a host of uniformed officers. The officers let him pass, strangely quiet for a seasoned group such as this.

Once inside the building, he followed the sounds and light escaping an open door. He inhaled deeply then held his breath before stepping into the long-deserted classroom. Blood splattered every surface.

"He's escalating," Dr. Graves whispered.

"Yeah." Detective Davis' pale face said it all.

Dr. Graves stopped just inside the door to put on shoe covers handed to him by a uniformed cop. He straightened up and swept his fingers through his hair. "Not just in decreased time between attacks, but in the intensity...the, the *savagery* of the attacks." He shook his head, a frown creasing his forehead.

He started his visual examination of the victim at his torso, clenching his jaw at the devastation—all done while the victim was alert but paralyzed. When his gaze fell on the victim's face, his heart stopped for several seconds and he swayed on his feet. He latched onto the arm of the forensics photographer standing next to him to keep from falling.

"You okay, doc?" Detective Fitzpatrick asked, stepping toward him.

Dr. Graves' throat had closed, he couldn't even drag in a breath, much less speak in that moment. His eyeballs, the pressure, they were going to explode right out of their sockets. He recognized that face. Friday. His flustered mind struggled to find the name of the bar.

"Do you need to sit down, Graves?" Detective Davis asked.

A shake of the head. Dr. Graves forced some air through his throat and into his lungs. He steadied himself before letting go of the photographer and looking straight at the two detectives. "I know this man. Or, I mean, I've seen him before. And I saw the killer." He ran his hands through his hair again and muttered, "The sober guy. It was the sober guy."

Every person in the room stood stark still, eyes pinned to the doctor.

He spun around, nearly toppling over with the speed of the move, and hurried out the door, down the hall, and outside, not stopping until he reached his car. He slammed his fist on the roof hard enough to leave a dent. He grasped the edge of the roof, knuckles blanching immediately, and lowered his head between his arms, muttering. "I knew something was off. No photos. I could have stopped him."

This death is on me.

Dr. Graves looked up at the sound of footsteps as Fitzpatrick and Davis approached. He pushed off his car and waved them away. "I'll meet you at the morgue." He needed to be alone with his thoughts. He got into his car before they could object and sped away.

BY THE TIME Kat arrived at the morgue, Dr. Graves had somewhat calmed down. His hair was sticking up all over due to the number of times he'd grabbed fistfuls of it in his anguish over his unyielding belief he could have prevented this murder. He paced next to the exam table where soon would lie the latest victim. The man from the bar Friday night. The one who'd sat right across from him, getting drunker as the night wore on and as the killer supplied him with drink after drink.

He closed his eyes and tried to picture the murderer's face.

"Dr. Graves?" Kat stepped through the door to the stairwell and stopped a few steps away from where he stood with his fingers wrapped in his tangled hair again. He dropped his hands and looked her direction, but he couldn't look her in the face. "What's wrong?" She stepped closer.

"There's been another murder," he croaked out, hanging his head low, his chin touching his chest.

"Oh no." She closed the gap between them and laid her hands on his shoulders. "Look at me." She narrowed her eyes when he complied. "There's something else, isn't there?"

He nodded, eyes cast down again. His voice broke as he told her, "I saw him. Saw *them*. On Friday. At the bar on Friday night."

Her grip on his shoulders tightened. "Um, wow. Dean"—it was the first time she'd used his given name in over a week—"take a slow, deep breath, then blow it out through your mouth. Do it five times."

The first breath hurt. His chest didn't want to expand, it held firm like a new balloon. The pain and tightness eased, and by the fifth breath, he felt he'd regained most of his composure. Kat's hands never left his shoulders, and now that his mind was clearer, he could feel that touch down to his toes.

"Better?" she asked.

He nodded.

"Good. Then start over."

"I saw the killer and the victim on Friday. They were sitting with a third guy in a booth just across from me." He twitched, just stopping himself from grabbing his hair again.

"How do you know which one was the killer?"

A slight tremor ran down his spine as it all clicked; as he realized what had been nagging at him. "The one that was sober. The one that kept ordering more drinks for the other two—especially for the victim. He was focused in on the victim, the other guy was just a nuisance to him, in the way of his target." That's what the nagging feeling he'd had there was trying to show him—the difference in the way the killer treated them. The well-disguised disdain in his eyes when he laughed at something the victim said. The hard liquor he ordered for the victim while ordering only beer for the third-wheel. The guy was having a hard time keeping his head up and his eyes open by the time Dr. Graves' headache had run him from the bar. "I should have known," he whispered.

Kat lifted her hands from his shoulders, and for a brief moment he felt that loss like his life-blood spilled to the floor. Then she stepped a little closer and took one of his hands, and the hemorrhaging stopped. "And if you had suspected then, on Friday? What would you have done?"

"Followed him."

Her fingernails dug into his palm as her grip tightened, but he didn't pull away. "Then I'm glad you didn't put the pieces together."

The service elevator dinged, and Kat let go of his hand.

"I would have called the police, too," he said as they started toward the opening doors of the elevator.

After the body bag had been moved to the exam table and Kat and Dr. Graves were left alone with the body, he said, "Bolster yourself, this one is horrific."

Kat cocked an eyebrow. "They've all been horrific."

He shook his head. "He's upped his viciousness factor by droves."

⎯᚜⎯

Save for one small break in the early afternoon, when Dr. Graves left to get a new phone activated, it took them twelve hours to do the autopsy and document the two-hundred plus wounds, none of which had been what killed the man.

Dr. Graves walked Kat to her car in the waning sunlight. Neither of them spoke; Kat just reached out and squeezed his hand, frowning and letting the trauma of the day show in her eyes.

Chief Billings called him on his way home. Without preamble, she said, "So, I hear that your reaction at the murder scene was interesting."

"Yeah, I suppose it was."

"Wanna tell me about it? And by that I mean, *tell me about it.*"

He sighed. "I'll give you the short version because it's been a long day. You can pick my brain about it tomorrow." He told her about his bar-gazing, as Kat had called it, and about seeing the trio Friday night.

"Okay. I'll let you be so you can go home and get some rest, but I will be talking to you about this activity of yours. And, I'm hoping to get some security camera footage from that bar for you to look at tomorrow, too. And if they don't have cameras, expect a visit from our sketch artist."

"Have an uneventful evening, Tracey." He sighed as he disconnected the call.

—\/—

Morning arrived all too early. Dr. Graves texted Kat: *I got the coffee today. See you at work.*

She replied: *Good, running late.*

And then: *Thank you.*

He sat in his car in the parking lot, head resting against his arms on the steering wheel, for several minutes. He'd never questioned his choice of profession before, but he was now. He'd never had to talk himself into getting out of the car and going into the office, except for today. Straightening up in his seat, he took a deep breath, sipped his coffee, then resignedly left the peace and quiet of his car.

Setting the coffee on his desk, he glanced at the pile of police reports in his basket, hoping he'd have time to get to them today. Not that it was going to make a difference to yesterday's victim. He bowed his head and clenched his fists so tight the muscles in his arms ached.

The elevator dinged. Dr. Graves rolled his shoulders and shook out his arms before trying to put on, if not a happy face, at least a neutral one.

Kat headed straight for the coffee on his desk and took a long drink before even talking. She had dark circles under her eyes, reminiscent of the ones he'd seen in the mirror that morning. This serial killer business was getting to her too. How could it not?

She closed her eyes and took in a deep breath before opening them and zoning in on him as he stood behind his desk. "What's on the agenda today, doctor?"

Looking down at the pile of folders, he said, "Why don't we get started on these. You take half and I'll take half."

She nodded, picking up half the folders with her left hand while balancing her coffee in the right. "Happy hump day," she murmured as she left.

Sighing, Dr. Graves looked up at the ultraviolet light, wishing suddenly that his office wasn't in the basement. He could really use some sunlight streaming through a window right then. He pulled his chair back, consciously compelling himself not to wrench it across the room. He plopped into the chair and slid the first missing person's file in front of him, determined to force himself to concentrate on the task at hand.

Nothing suspicious jumped out at him. The man didn't fit the killer's profile and, besides, he went missing while hiking alone in the forest. He was probably nothing but a pile of bones and scat on the forest floor by now.

The phone rang and Dr. Graves' heart skipped like a stone over a pond. He was starting to feel like he had PTSD every time he heard the stupid ring tone. Always bad news lately.

"Dr. Graves," he answered warily.

"Hey, Dean." Tracey's voice was solemn. "We got the footage

from the security cameras at that bar. Can you come down to the station and point this guy out to us?"

"Yeah." He scrunched his eyes closed and rubbed his forehead. "He'll be the one with the victim."

"Was that sarcasm I heard, Dr. Graves?" the Chief of Police asked.

He sighed. "Yeah, maybe. Sorry, Tracey. I'll be there in a few minutes."

Kat met him in the hallway, holding a folder in her outstretched hand. "I may have found something."

"Good. I have to go up to the station; you can tell me about it when I get back."

She pulled the folder against her chest and nodded. "Okay. I wanted to check a few things out anyway. See you when you get back."

TWENTY SIX

Nine Months Ago
Carter, age 27

Ten years.

Ten years since *he* had killed Carter's little brother. Cody would be twenty-two now, just starting his life.

Ten years since *he* had killed Carter's mom. Carter couldn't remember what her voice sounded like. He did remember her last words to him, though: "We're running a little late, but we'll be there. I'm so proud of you. Love you." She'd left that message on Carter's cell just before his high school graduation ceremony started. Oh, how he wished he wouldn't have deleted it right after listening to it.

He watched from the back of the parking lot outside the fence of the Washington State Prison in Davisboro.

Right on time, the gates opened, and *he* walked out, dressed in street clothes and carrying a small bag. The Dick hadn't aged, still had the same annoying swagger and messy brown hair. The only difference Carter could see from a distance was that the murderer stepped with surety, no wobbling or swaying. Sober.

Carter closed his eyes and took slow, deep breaths to control the fury building inside him. Fresh rage on top of the constant rage he'd been carrying with him ever since that night. He gripped the steering wheel, knuckles turning white. He pictured those hands—his own hands, yet somehow seeming a separate part from him, a separate entity—circling the man's neck, the knuckles white from the pressure of strangling him, snapping his cricoid cartilage as he watched the life drain from the man's eyes. But that would be too merciful.

Snapped out of his fantasy, Carter watched as a cab pulled up and The Dick slid into the back seat. Carter let the cab get a head start then pulled out of the parking lot and followed it at a distance for over an hour, back into Augusta.

The cab stopped in front of the Augusta Transitional Center.

Carter narrowed his eyes, watching from the street, his breathing unsteady as The Dick made his way inside the shabby single-story, red brick building. *Living in a halfway house would make it a little more difficult to get The Dick alone...*

But Carter had a plan.

—⋀—

THREE MONTHS AGO
Carter, age 28

HE'D WAITED six months to set his plan in motion. The wait had seemed longer than the past ten years because he knew he could've so easily grabbed The Dick at any time. But he played it smart because he didn't want to get caught. He forced himself to wait until Dickwad got his own apartment. Then he waited until after The Dick had met with his probation officer. Carter made sure the murderer would "quit" his job before Monday and did some research to find out that The Dick's brother—his only living relative—had died in a construction accident a few years back. No one would miss him for at least a few months.

Carter had slipped a note under his apartment door a week ago, inviting him to dinner:

Richard,

It's been a long time. I'd like to offer a reconciliation between the two of us. I've found religion and realize a need to forgive you.

—Carter rolled his eyes as he wrote that. There was no god. Just men with power and men without—

Please come to dinner at my house, where we can talk, next Friday, 6:00. I'll come pick you up.
    Carter

Carter gripped his steering wheel as the man who killed his mom and brother walked toward his car.

—⋀—

HE SLIPPED a strong sedative into Dick-wad's diet cola and acted the part of reformed hater, now forgiver until it took effect. He stripped Dick-wad, laid his flaccid body on the table, and used tie-downs to restrain him. He started an IV in the man's arm and gave him an antidote to the sedative before meticulously laying out his instruments. Then he paced, waiting for the antidote to take effect. His hands trembled, not with fear but with excitement. He didn't even question whether this was the right thing to do, to take a life. The thought never even crossed his mind in any serious way, just a flickering wonderment that it was so. His mind buzzed with a sort of ecstasy that extended out to his fingertips and toes like little electric impulses.

It wasn't a question of right or wrong. Killing this man was *meant to be.*

Dick-wad shuddered and his eyes flew open. "What the—"

"Hey! You're awake. Good." Carter looked down into confused eyes.

"What...what are you doing?"

"Revenge. Justice." Carter connected the syringe full of succinylcholine to the IV port and depressed the plunger as he continued. "I've waited so long for this."

The ET tube went in smoothly. Carter's hand shook as he forced himself to work slowly, to draw out the pain. With the knife's first slash into the Dick-wad's tender belly, as the blood pooled around the incision, Carter's heart fluttered and his fingers ached to go faster. "You have all night," he reminded himself with a whisper. He interrupted the torture to breathe for the paralyzed man with an ambu bag, then resumed, cutting down to the intestines. He pulled a loop out, crushed it in his shaking hand, then laid it on Dick-wad's torso before the succs wore off.

With bloody fingers, Carter removed the ET tube from his stepdad's throat, holding his breath with anticipation as he stared into the man's terror-filled eyes.

As soon as the tube cleared his vocal cords, Dick-wad screamed. The sound of it penetrated straight to Carter's soul, and he laughed with sheer joy.

"Please...stop. Carter, please—" His words cut off with a shriek when Carter yanked on the exposed intestines.

Tears streamed down the sides of Dick's face as he panted. He begged with a trembling voice, "The accident wasn't my fault! C-Carter, listen to me! Your mom wouldn't want you to do this! C-Cody wouldn't want you to do this!"

An explosion ripped through Carter's mind. His tightly held fury erupted, and he plunged his knife into Richard's neck, nearly severing his head from it. "How dare you speak their names!"

—⌁—

"DAMNIT!" Carter slammed his fist into the wall, punching through the drywall. He'd killed him too fast. The abuser hadn't suffered enough. Carter had followed his plan to perfection up to that point. Sedated him. Paralyzed him. Intubated him. Cut him. When the paralytic wore off...the shrieks were orgasmic to Carter's ears. The restrained, bleeding man begged—like Cody used to when the grown-ass bully beat him.

Carter buried him in his garden, the soft Georgia soil complying to each thrust of the shovel. Tears flowed for the first time since graduation night as he dug, but this time they were borne of pure rage, not a combination of anger and grief like before. *This was supposed to be the end of it! This was supposed to fix it all! Righteous vengeance for Cody and my mom!*

He'd done it too fast. He hadn't made the murderer suffer enough.

As he shoveled soil over the body, an idea slammed into his head.

An *epiphany*.

The only way to avenge his brother and mom was to kill again. Only, next time, he'd do it right.

TWENTY SEVEN

PRESENT DAY
Dr. Graves

Dr. Graves was gone longer than he'd planned. It took a while to find the right camera angle and then forward it to the right time of night. They didn't get a good look at the killer's face, he had a baseball cap pulled low over his forehead. They chose the best few stills they could get and sent them off to the FBI to enter into their facial recognition program.

The smell of the fresh donuts he'd stopped to get on his way back wafted through the elevator and his head. If ever he needed some comfort food, it was today. Kat met him almost at the elevator doors as they opened, not quite a smile on her face, but there was a twinkle in her eyes.

"You found something," he said.

She nodded.

He followed her to her office and set the box of donuts on a chair as she went around to the other side of her desk. "This guy"—she shook the file in her hand—"fits the profile. His actual date of disappearance is unknown—the report was only filed by his probation officer a couple of weeks ago because he'd missed two check-ins. The last time he was seen by anyone was about three months ago."

The donuts lay forgotten as Dr. Graves bent forward, nodding.

Kat continued, "I called his P.O. and asked about his history."

Now she leaned in and their faces were only a foot apart across her desk. "He has a wife and stepson buried at the cemetery..."

"*The* cemetery?" Dr. Graves interrupted. "The one where we found the second victim?"

"Yes! And that's not all. I dug a little deeper to see if he had any connections to the other two places."

"And?"

She turned her monitor toward him. He wasn't sure what he was looking at. An old class photo? He looked up at her, brows furrowed.

She pointed to a boy in the back row. "That's him. That's this guy"—she tapped the folder—"He went there as a kid, the school from yesterday."

Dr. Graves inched closer to the screen and stared at the boy in the image. "And the house?" he whispered.

"He grew up there."

He grabbed her hand and straightened up. "This is it. He was the first victim."

Nodding, Kat squeezed his hand. "He has a stepson. A nurse anesthetist." She smiled grimly. "I have a name, Dean. He—"

"You can tell me the rest later. I need to call Tracey."

—◠—

"Shit." Fitzpatrick slammed his fist on Chief Billings' desk. He pressed on his closed eyelids with shaking fingers as he growled, "We interviewed this guy. Weeks ago."

Tracey narrowed her eyes and said through thinned lips, "Then you should know where to find him. Go."

The two detectives spun and left the office without another word.

With a sigh big enough to open a sail, Tracey set her eyes on Dr. Graves. "We'll have him in custody before the end of the day—" She paused, then muttered, "I hope."

Dr. Graves let his shoulders sag in front of his friend, too exhausted to keep his posture in line any longer. "I hope so too."

TWENTY EIGHT

Present Day
Carter, age 28

The receptionist at the same-day surgical center smiled up at Carter as he laid a hand on her shoulder. She touched his bicep and licked her lips. She wanted him. They all did. He flexed his muscles for her, and her breath caught with a slight gasp.

The entrance door-chimes dinged and he looked up; his hand tightened, digging into the tender tissue between the receptionist's shoulder and collar bone for a heartbeat as his guts roiled in a maelstrom of hate. Cops. Plain-clothed cops with badges hanging from lanyards around their necks.

"Shit," Carter sneered under his breath. As the girl twisted around to see what he'd been looking at, he rushed into the back.

"How can I help you?" she asked as the staff door swung closed.

Carter stood on the other side of the door, listening. They couldn't be there for *him*. He was worrying for nothing.

"I'm Detective Fitzpatrick and this is Detective Davis." He paused. "We need to speak with Carter Ridge."

"Oh..."

The rest of her response was lost as Carter spun and speed-walked past the nurses' station, heading for the staff locker room.

Lily, one of the nurses, called out, "Hey, Carter, Dr. Dorman's case is about to start."

But he didn't slow his step or even look in her direction.

Carter swept through the door and locked it behind him. It had never been locked for as long as he'd worked there. He hoped that meant they didn't have a key or at least didn't know where it was. He spun the padlock on his locker and cursed as he went past the second number and had to start over. On the third try, it opened. He threw the lock behind him and pulled up on the lever to open the locker.

The door to the staff room rattled behind him, followed by the receptionist's voice. "Um... Lily? This door is locked. Do we even have a key?"

Carter grabbed his bag from the bottom of the locker, lifted his street clothes from the hooks, and shoved his hand in the pants' pocket as he headed for the back door. He pulled his keys out as he stepped into the parking lot, nearly dropping them as he fumbled to push the unlock button while jogging to his SUV.

"Shit!" He glanced over his shoulder at the door he'd just come through. No one had followed him out. Good.

He climbed into the vehicle and tore out of the parking lot without even buckling his seatbelt. His heart raced, and he nearly ran the stop sign at the end of the street, slamming on the brakes and skidding to a stop a foot or so beyond the sign. "Get it together," he whispered. He took a steadying breath, put his seat belt on to stop the incessant dinging, and with the appearance of complete calmness— even though the pressure in his chest had built to an unbearable mass —pulled onto the road, heading for the freeway.

TWENTY NINE

Present Day
Dr. Graves

Dr. Graves slammed his phone back onto the receiver, grabbed his Avengers mug and hurled it at the wall across from his desk with a primal growl. Shards of ceramic danced with pens as they fell to the floor. Dr. Graves dropped his head into his hands, his fingers twisted in his hair.

The door to his office flew open, slamming against the wall hard enough to bounce it back toward Kat. She stopped it with the palm of her hand, a worried scowl creasing her face. "Are you okay?" She looked from him to the mess on the floor. "What happened?"

With a huge sigh he lowered his hands to the desk, staring down at them but seeing nothing. "He got away. The detectives went in the front door, and he slipped out the back."

Kat's shoulders slumped as she trudged to the chair facing his desk, lowering herself into it. "So...what now? They have his name and everything, so they should be able to find him. Right?" Pleading haunted that last word.

He looked up at her, trying to smooth the worry lines from his face. "They put out an APB, put tracers on his credit cards, and got a search warrant for his house. They're there now."

"They'll find him," Kat whispered. "They have to."

—⋀—

"I'M ONLY SHARING this information with you two because you've been an integral part of this investigation." Chief Billings looked at Dr. Graves and Kat in turn, a stern eyebrow raised. "No one else is to know this—especially not the press."

They nodded, both frozen in place where they stood out in the morgue. Before the very same cold metal table where they'd painstakingly assessed and documented the hundreds of wounds inflicted on three of the killer's victims.

"Mr. Ridge kept some souvenirs." Tracey set four clear plastic bags on the table. "One from each victim."

"Four?" Kat asked, staring at the bags.

Tracey nodded. "Yeah. We think you two were right and that one of these items belonged to the stepdad."

Dr. Graves stepped closer to the table, and after a quick perusal of the items, picked one of the bags up, bringing it closer to his face. "It's this one." He held it up for Kat to see as Tracey nodded.

"What is it?" Kat narrowed her eyes at the object. "Some sort of coin?"

"It's a sobriety chip. Ten years. He was an alcoholic, as I suspected." He looked up at Kat. "What did you say he was serving time for?"

"Vehicular homicide. He had a BAC of 1.9 and swerved into the side of a semi. Killed his wife and her twelve-year-old son instantly. He barely had a scratch."

"How old would our suspect have been at the time?" Tracey asked.

"He was eighteen. They were on their way to his high school graduation." Kat sighed. "Instead of his mom and brother greeting him after the ceremony, he was met by two officers delivering the news."

"Tragic," Dr. Graves said, voice stiff, "but no excuse for what he's done. What he's going to do again if we don't catch him soon."

"You really think he'll strike again soon?" Chief Billings asked. "I figure he'll hole up, go into hiding for a while now that he knows we're onto him."

"We can only hope that's the case." Dr. Graves dropped the bag holding the sobriety chip back onto the table. "But I don't know... He's been spiraling, and I have a feeling this little setback won't make any difference to his deranged mind." He looked up at the Chief of Police. "In fact, I think it may make him frenzied. Like a tank full of sharks after a bloodied animal is dropped in."

THIRTY

Carter Ridge's 4Runner was found Thursday morning, stashed in a forested area just off a little two-lane highway not far from Augusta. No sign of the killer or how he was traveling now.

Well, Dr. Graves thought, *I found him once before, I'll find him again. And this time I know what he looks like.*

He powered up his computer, determination all that kept him awake after a sleepless night, and searched for other abandoned buildings and out-of-the-way places that might be associated with the killer's stepdad. Would the killer stick to his modus operandi even though he'd almost been caught? It was the only thing Dr. Graves could think of to narrow down the list of bars he would need to check out. He found a few places that had definite brushes with the stepdad's life and searched bars in those areas—and narrowed the list further by choosing those beyond the city and in the direction the 4Runner had been found.

He locked his screen and covered his written list with his hand when Kat came through the door to his office, balancing a Styrofoam cup in each hand. "I figured you'd need this today."

He smiled as he flipped the legal pad over—trying to look casual about it. But, Kat raised an eyebrow and pursed her lips. "Thank you," he said, before she could comment on the notebook. "I don't think I slept a wink."

"Yeah"—she eyed him suspiciously—"me either."

He needed to give her something to do, to get her off his trail. "The DA emailed this morning. He's already preparing his case in anticipation of the police catching up with Mr. Ridge. He wants us to go over our reports with a fine-toothed comb, as he put it. Will you please read over them carefully, and doublecheck for any misspellings, typos, or inconsistencies?"

"Didn't you already do that, like always?"

He took a sip of his coffee. "Well, yes. Of course. But I'd like you to go over them anyway, in case I missed anything. Two sets of eyes are better than one."

"Of course, I'll get started right away." She gave the downturned legal pad one more glance before she turned and walked out.

Dr. Graves watched her leave with a strange flutter in his chest. His lips twitched as if they were thinking about smiling, but he crushed that thought as he turned back to his notepad. He sent a quick email to Tracey with the list of possible future murder sites he'd compiled, though he knew they didn't have the manpower to watch them all.

Tonight, he would go scope out The Rusty Duck. He'd have to leave right after work as it was a long drive, probably take him two or two-and-a-half hours, maybe longer if he hit rush hour traffic. But he had to do something. Dr. Graves couldn't shake the feeling that the killer was going to strike again, soon, no matter what Tracey thought. He was at the point in his psychotic fixation that he couldn't put the brakes on; the urge to kill again would only be growing stronger as each day passed. And he didn't even have his job to distract him now.

THURSDAY NIGHT HAD BEEN A BUST. The Rusty Duck had turned out to be no more than a shack with a few barstools spread out across a dirty bar. It hadn't been worth the sleep deprivation. And, as he'd suspected, Tracey had responded to his email with little hope. She'd called the local police departments in the areas of the places he'd given her, and they said they would increase patrols near those sites and neighboring bars. It wasn't going to be enough to catch Ridge, though. Dr. Graves laid his head on his arms at his desk and drifted off.

He didn't hear Kat's approach down the hall from her office. She cleared her throat from a distance, and he jerked to a sitting position, finding her at his door. "I...uhh...finished going over those reports," she said.

"Thank you. How did they look?"

"Pristine, as usual. I can't say the same for you." She walked over to his desk, narrowing her eyes as she studied him. "You look awful."

He shrugged. "I just need an extra shot of caffeine. Sleep has been an evasive friend lately."

"Yeah, I get that." Kat sighed.

The doctor realized an opportunity here. "I think I might take off a little early today. Try to get some rest."

Kat's face shifted to an unreadable, stiff expression. "That's not a bad idea. You definitely look like you can use it."

She suspects something. Of course she does; I never leave early. But that couldn't be helped. He *had* to find Carter Ridge. The thought of doing one more autopsy of one of his victims was enough to send Dr. Graves to an early retirement.

He pulled the list of bars out of his desk drawer and crossed off The Rusty Duck. Not knowing where the killer had run to, he couldn't make a logical decision about which bar to go to next. So, he just chose the next one on the list, writing "Fri" next to it before moving on to the following one and writing "Sat." He continued down the list like this, hoping with all his might he wouldn't get past tonight. Shenanigans would be another two-hour drive. At least he could sleep-in tomorrow.

–\/–

At least Shenanigans had a bar *and* tables. It was smaller than the pubs in the city, but it didn't smell of urine and mold like The Rusty Duck had. And it did a booming business for residing in such a small town. But, in the standing-room-only Friday night crowd, Dr. Graves saw no sign of the killer. He sighed and took another sip of his water, scanning the room for the hundredth time.

"Can I buy you a drink? Something besides that boring glass of water you've been nursing all night?"

Dr. Graves, too tired to startle at the interruption, squinted up at the tall woman wearing a very short, very tight red dress that left nothing to the imagination. He twisted his lips into a half-hearted smile. "No, thank you. I'm actually leaving soon."

She slid into the chair opposite his and pushed her bottom lip out into a pout, setting her drink on the table. "Aw, don't be like that. The party's just getting started." She leaned in, exposing even more of her cleavage, and laid a hand on top of his. "Or we could move the party somewhere else. Somewhere private." She winked.

Pulling his hand out from under hers, he said sternly, "That is a very dangerous proposition, ma'am. You don't even know my name. I could be a serial killer, for all you know." He became even more uptight when exhausted, apparently. He internally groaned at himself for lecturing a complete stranger. But he wasn't wrong.

"*Are* you a serial killer?" She slurred a little and smiled. Not deterred by his fatherly advice.

"Well, of course not. But you don't know that." He scowled.

"Oh, I have a sick...sixth sense about these things. You're as harmless as a mouse. And as handsome as a movie star." She reached for him again.

Dr. Graves jerked his hand away as her fingers brushed his, spilling her drink. Her reaction was slow, and the pungent liquid spread across the table and dripped down onto her dress before she moved out of the way. He grabbed a handful of napkins from the dispenser at the end of the table and stood, stepping around to her side just as she finally got her muscles moving. She pushed up from the chair and swayed toward him, looking down at her dress. He held out the napkins as she looked back up at him. She stood only an inch or two shorter than him. She took the napkins and slowly rubbed at the spot on her dress, her eyes never leaving his. The tip of her tongue snaked out and traced her upper lip.

The way she was rubbing those napkins on herself...well, heat flashed up Dr. Graves' neck and head. The woman smiled and with a moan, dropped the napkins to the floor and embraced him with the quickness of a cheetah. Her lips pressed against his faster than he could blink. It must have been the shock of the moment that kept him from immediately pulling away. That and the wrestler's grip she held him in.

His brain malfunctioned like a glitchy computer. Kat's face filled his inner vision, and for a moment he believed it was her lips pressed to his. And a split second after he realized it wasn't her, he wished it was. Knew he wanted it to be Kat. He jolted away from the very forward woman and mumbled, "Sorry about your dress. I...I must leave now." He swiped his sleeve across his mouth as he hurried to the door, shame and confusion welling up inside him.

He needn't have been afraid of dozing off on the long drive home —his mind wouldn't stop racing. What had that been? The thing with Kat's image popping into his head at such an inappropriate moment. He needed to get some sleep.

THIRTY ONE

Present Day
Dr. Graves

Home in bed, Dr. Graves' mind still wouldn't give it a break. So he did something he'd never done before—he took two diphenhydramine tablets even though he was having zero allergic symptoms. He finally dozed off around four o'clock in the morning.

At ten-thirty he stared out his kitchen window, waiting for his coffee to finish brewing. His phone buzzed and he froze, an icy chill pirouetting up his spine, until he realized the single buzz signaled a text message. The detectives wouldn't text to tell him about another victim; they'd call. He poured coffee into his mug and took a sip, burning his tongue, before looking at his phone.

It was Kat. His stomach twitched when he saw her name, and he set his mug down with a clank, the memory of her invasion into his mind last night hitting him full force. He squeezed his eyes shut and forced a deep breath into his constricted lungs, willing the image from his mind and scolding himself for losing control. He looked at her message: *Did you get some sleep?*

He bit the inside of his cheek, oddly emotional that she thought to ask.

He texted back: *Yes, more than I have been. How about you?*

Kat: *Yes. It's amazing what a glass—or three—of wine will do to help in that area.*

Dr. Graves: *I'm glad you found something to help.*

Kat: *Dean. You aren't doing anything dangerous, are you? I'm worried about you.*

His thumbs hovered over the phone's virtual keyboard. He didn't want to lie to her, but he also didn't want her to try to talk him out of it. And he most assuredly didn't want her to tag along—it *was* too dangerous. He rolled his shoulders and stretched his neck side-to-side. He decided he'd have to be blunt; that was his natural inclination anyway. It came easy to him.

Dr. Graves: *Stop worrying about me. I can take care of myself.*

The three dots appeared on his screen to show Kat was typing something. Then they disappeared. Several seconds later they popped up again. Then disappeared.

Dr. Graves lifted his coffee mug off the counter and went out onto his back deck. He sat down and placed his phone, screen down, on the small table beside him. He took another drink of his coffee then held the warm mug in his hands as he rested his head against the back of the chair, closing his eyes while the cool morning breeze tickled his skin.

When his phone buzzed again several minutes later, he didn't immediately pick it up. He continued his silent meditation, the scent of coffee soothing him.

The distinct call of a cardinal in the distance brought his head forward and his eyes open. He sighed and lifted his phone from beside him.

Kat: *K*

A one letter response. That probably wasn't a good sign. He set the phone back down and distracted himself by gazing into the trees, searching for the cardinal. He'd find a way to make it up to her later.

—⋀—

GRAVEL CRUNCHED under his tires as he pulled into the parking lot. With a name like Odin's Beard, Dr. Graves had expected the place to at least have a paved parking lot. Small and large puddles dotted the depressions in the graveled surface, thanks to the downpour this afternoon. The rain had stopped, but the clouds lingered, obscuring the stars. He noted only one light pole in the lot, the light of which barely pierced the surrounding darkness with a dim yellow glow.

The place wasn't exactly hopping based on the number of cars parked near him. But it seemed busy enough. He exited his car and locked the doors with his key fob before shoving both it and his phone into his pocket. He hated walking on gravel. Little pieces always got stuck in the tread of his shoes, and he'd have to dig them out later.

The parking lot had been somewhat deceiving, he thought, as he pushed through the door. There were more people in there than he'd expected. He found a seat at the bar and ordered his usual, water with no ice, and he added on a plate of nachos to keep the accountants happy.

The bartender set his water on a small cardboard disk then slid a plate of nachos in front of him. Dr. Graves pulled a chip from the pile and, after fighting with the string of cheese coming along for the ride, he put the whole thing in his mouth. He crunched it between his teeth while he observed his surroundings—or rather, the people surrounding him. He stopped mid-chew and leaned forward, his heart stuttering to a stop in his chest.

He's here.

At the other end of the bar.

He stared right into Dr. Graves' eyes.

Dr. Graves inhaled sharply, aspirating bits of tortilla chip into his lungs. He lost sight of the killer as he coughed himself into a tracheolaryngeal spasm that refused entrance of any air into his lungs for several seconds. When he somewhat recovered, tears streaming from his eyes, he whipped his head back and forth, searching for Carter Ridge. He reached for his phone, dragging it from his pocket as he continued to search through the crowd.

He glanced down and for a moment forgot which button to push in order to make a phone call. Finding the right one, he pressed it and then hit the 9. The phone flew from his hand before he could hit the

1, swatted away by a beefy hand. He looked up—and met the gaze of the killer. Dr. Graves' heart hiccoughed, a sharp pain grabbing his chest. Carter Ridge retrieved the phone from the floor and booked it to the exit.

"Call the police!" the doctor yelled to the bartender before running after the killer. He didn't stop to see if his directive was obeyed as he slammed through the door. With a quick glance at the parking lot, he decided to run for his car so he could follow the murderer—assuming the man would flee. Trying to stay aware of his surroundings, he jogged toward his car while digging his key out of his pocket. He clicked to unlock it and reached for the handle as soon as he skidded up next to it.

Pain ripped through his skull, and he slunk to his knees as a loud thump echoed through his head. Still aware, but unable to make his muscles obey, he watched as Carter Ridge, with the expertise of his profession, stabbed a needle into Dr. Graves' antecubital vein and depressed the plunger of the attached syringe. He didn't even have time to consider what the drug was as he slipped into unconsciousness.

THIRTY TWO

Present Day
Dr. Graves

Concrete.

As he assessed his surroundings, Dr. Graves turned his head and nearly cried out at the sharp pain that stabbed at his brain.

Bars.

Light. A heavy-duty flashlight hung from a dangling wire in the ceiling.

Where was he? The scent of dust and mold assaulted him. He moved to cover his nose, but stopped short. His hands were restrained. He tested his legs to find that they were as well. So tight were the restraints that his hands and feet had gone numb.

Footsteps echoed on a hard surface and terror such as he'd never experienced overwhelmed him as snippets of the killer's victims flashed through his mind. "No," he whispered.

The footsteps grew closer, and Dr. Graves' heart pounded against his ribs with rapid percussion. The pressure grew in his chest until he thought it would explode. A fleeting thought crossed through the panic—maybe he'd die of a myocardial infarction before the killer could torture him.

"Well, hello there, Mr. Graves," Carter said as he stepped up to the table Dr. Graves was strapped to.

"*Doctor* Graves." The reprimand broke from his mouth by pure reflex.

"*Doctor*... I almost expected it to be *Officer* or *Detective*, by the recognition in your eyes back there at the bar."

"How do you know my name?"

Carter rolled his eyes and held up the doctor's wallet. "How did *you* know who *I* was, *doctor*?"

Dr. Graves swallowed, trying to keep the quiver from his voice. "Let's just say I've seen your work, Mr. Ridge." Images swept over him, and he shuddered and squeezed his eyes shut. He had to figure a way out of this. "I..." He swallowed again. "I'm a little surprised to be here, Mr. Ridge. I'm not your usual victim. I don't even drink alcohol."

Carter smiled. It would have been a pleasant smile on his handsome face if not for the madness behind his eyes. "Good for you. Alcohol is a foul poison, makes people do bad things." He moved close, staring directly down into Dr. Graves' eyes. "You definitely weren't my first choice, but you were going to ruin it. You were going to call the police. And I'm not finished with the reckoning yet."

"Maybe, since I don't fit your profile, you would consider just killing me quickly? I'm not naïve enough to believe you'll let me go, but..."

Carter laughed bitterly, the maniacal sound sending icicles into the innermost reaches of Dr. Graves' brain. "Oh, no, *Doctor* Graves. I enjoy my methods far too much for that. Plus, doctors have always treated me as *less than*, even though I do the same work as the anesthesiologists, *better* work. I'm not one of them. So, blame your stuffy colleagues for the suffering that is to come for you. Or don't. I really don't think it would matter if you were Mother Theresa; I'd still draw this out nice and slow."

A tear slipped down the side of Dr. Graves' face as bile rose in his throat. What had his last text to Kat been? Oh yeah. *I can take care of myself.* His hands closed into fists, his jaw clamped so tight he was sure he'd break multiple teeth. But what did it matter, really?

"Unfortunately," Carter said, dropping Dr. Graves' wallet onto his chest, "I won't be able to start right away. I need to go get some supplies, seeing as how I had to abandon my stash earlier this week, and I wasn't expecting another subject to fall right into my hands so soon."

Dr. Graves couldn't have responded had he wanted to. His throat constricted to the point that air barely wheezed through.

"Oh," Carter said in a mocking voice, "I see that you're disappointed in the delay. I suppose I could break protocol just this once. It'll give you something to think about while I'm gone." Again, the supermodel smile that didn't even come near to reaching his cold, predator eyes.

Instinct wouldn't let Dr. Graves keep his eyes closed, no matter how much his mind screamed at him to do so. He watched, shaking his head, as the monster raised an iron bar high and smashed it down onto Dr. Graves' left forearm, crushing the bones. Before the doctor could pull in enough air to scream at the pain, Carter moved down to his left lower leg, smashing the bar down again, shattering his tibia and fibula.

The killer pulled the flashlight down and unhooked it. He aimed the beam across the doctor's face, but not directly into his eyes.

Carter leaned in and waited for Dr. Graves to meet his gaze. "I'll see you in the morning, *doctor*. Have a fun night." He turned as if to leave but spun around and slammed the bar across Dr. Graves' lower chest, knocking the air out of him and likely cracking multiple ribs. The iron bar clanged to the ground as Dr. Graves fought to draw a breath.

Laughter—and the illumination from the flashlight—followed Carter out of the room.

⎯⋀⎯

Shock. He was going into shock. He may only work with deceased patients, but that didn't mean he didn't remember his training from medical school.

A cold sweat covered his forehead, then, everywhere, he realized.

His pulse accelerated. Was his chest pain from the rib injury or was he dying? His breaths came in short, rapid gasps until his head swam and his hands tingled, then his lips and face grew numb. He should do something, but he couldn't think through the pain, like shards of glass scissoring through his bones with each slight movement.

Nausea rolled through him.

No.

Vomiting was not a good idea.

His ribs.

More pain.

No.

Slow the breathing. That's what he needed to do. He drew in a breath through his nose then blew out through his mouth with a shaky, pathetic whimper. It didn't work. He was suffocating! The rapid breaths returned, and the nausea intensified. His heart pulsed out of control.

He rolled his head to the side and retched, spilling the contents of his stomach to pool beside him on the wide table, some dripping to whatever surface lay below, some soaking into his hair and shirt. Stabbing pain from his ribs rolled through him, and he vomited again before he could even take a breath. Agony threw his well-organized mind into chaos.

This was only the beginning.

Just a few broken bones.

He couldn't stop himself from picturing what he knew lay ahead. The *cutting* and the *burning* and the *disembowelment*. All while aware and paralyzed. A breathing tube down his throat.

He needed to pull himself together and figure out a way to get out of there.

Deal with the shock first. Dr. Graves closed his eyes. The strewn-out intestines of the second victim flashed in his mind, his eyes flew open, and he turned his head to the side to vomit once again. He clenched his jaw against the pain. *Think of something else.* Kat. Her face, her smile, her laugh, her intelligence.

He closed his eyes again, his mind firmly engaged with memories of Kat. He took slower, deeper breaths until his pulse slowed from that of a rabbit to that of a man running from a tornado. Then continued until it slowed to a man with several broken bones and no way to escape the terror to come.

THIRTY THREE

PRESENT DAY
Dr. Graves

The night—at least he assumed it was night—lasted for years but was over in a flash. Dr. Graves, in the pitch-black darkness, had tried everything he could think of to release his bindings. The blood around his right, unfractured wrist and ankle had gone from slippery, to sticky, to cracked and dry as it clotted and dried after he'd given up his struggle with the restraints. It was useless. He'd even tried rocking back and forth, hoping to tip the metal table over and possibly break it or find a way to cut off the bindings once on the ground. But the table was sturdy and wide and all he'd managed to do was increase his pain to the point of near syncope. Then he lay there, wishing, hoping, praying he'd pass out. Or die. He didn't *want* to die. But the alternative...

...it was going to end that way anyway.

All he did for hours, it seemed, was close his eyes and breathe, concentrating on the movement of air in and out of his lungs, a sharp pain stabbing at his ribs each time. The pungent odor of his vomit and the sick smell of fear tore into his nostrils with each inhale.

Footsteps. His breath hitched and all his muscles tensed at once, sending white-hot pokers into his broken bones and nerve endings. The footsteps neared, accompanied by humming. *Here Comes the Sun*. He hated The Beatles. His heart pounded like a locomotive, the thumping in his ears almost snuffing out the sound of his killer's steps and off-key humming.

Dr. Graves' eyes roved in circles as he waited for the man to reach him. He knew there was no way out, but his nervous system took over. Fight or flight. He could do neither, but the adrenaline shooting through his body apparently didn't know that.

"Well, good morning, Dr. Graves!" Carter plopped a heavy duffle bag on Dr. Graves' chest, forcing a half-moan, half-cry from his throat. As he stringed the flashlight back up above him, he said, "I hope you slept well. I didn't sleep a wink. I was too busy collecting supplies." He laughed. "Not as easy as it was last week when I was still working at the surgical center."

Dr. Graves' mind flew into hyper-speed. How could he get out of this? All he had available to him were words. "Carter," he rasped. "I know what your stepdad did. I'm sorry. What a horrible thing to deal with at such a young age."

Carter slammed his fist down on Dr. Graves' nose, smashing it. Fresh pain exploded into his face and skull.

"Don't! Don't talk about my family!" The killer unzipped the duffle bag and started pulling things out, laying some things on top of Dr. Graves' lap and legs, some to the side of the table, and some he just threw on the ground. "That drunk bastard killed my mom and little brother! And he walked away. Smashed their side of the car. *Decapitated* my mom." He shook his head and bellowed like a wild animal. "And his side looked untouched."

Dr. Graves didn't respond. Blood poured down his throat from his nose, and he could think of nothing except drawing in his next breath without drowning on it.

Leaning over the top of his victim, Carter growled, "Don't. Talk. About. My. Family."

The doctor closed his eyes, his pulse pounding in his broken nose, and shook his head. He was done talking. There was nothing he could do to save himself. Tears leaked down the sides of his face.

"No more talking. It's time to get started." The killer's face transformed from rage to cruel delight, a fevered grin spreading across it. Taking a pair of trauma shears, he cut off the doctor's clothes then pulled them unceremoniously out from under him and threw them into a corner of the room. He started an IV in Dr. Graves' unbroken arm and connected it to a bag of fluids. Glancing at the bloodied wrist, he laughed. "I'm an expert with restraints. Nice try, though."

The killer donned a white jumpsuit—like something a house painter might wear—shoe covers, and surgical gloves.

Dr. Graves watched through watering eyes, shivering as he lay naked on the cold metal table, while the killer grabbed a vial and plunged a needle into it, pulling the medication into the syringe. The thought of the detectives, Tracey...Kat, seeing him unclothed and bloody when they found his body flashed through his mind. And, even through the pain and terror, his psyche flushed with embarrassment.

Holding the syringe up to the light, Carter flicked it with his middle finger then squirted the air out. He repeated this process three more times, lining the four syringes up on the table next to Dr. Graves' thigh. He connected one of the syringes to the IV tubing, clamping it off above so the medication would flow into Dr. Graves and not the bag of fluids. "Now for the fun part."

"Carter..."

Ridge bared his teeth like a predator and pushed the plunger on the syringe, emptying the entire thing into Dr. Graves' vein. "No more talking."

"Please, listen. Please don't..." His mouth stopped cooperating as the paralysis hit him. Everything went slack and his chest stopped rising and falling with breaths. His eyelids remained half opened, but he couldn't even move his eyes, they were fixed on the ceiling above. Panic flooded him as his mind demanded his body to breathe, to move, to react—and nothing happened. Nothing. The rapidly increasing heart rate pounding in his chest was his only reaction. The paralytics didn't affect the heart. He screamed internally, making no sound. The blood from his nose pooled in the back of his throat. The need to take a breath overwhelmed all else. Yet, his body refused.

Carter now stood at the crown of his head, intubation tools in hand. He tilted the doctor's head back and inserted a laryngoscope deep into his mouth. It pushed against the base of his tongue where it connected to his throat, the pressure increasing as Carter rocked the scope back to pry his bottom jaw up and open. As he peered into the doctor's throat, he commentated aloud, "Gonna have to go in blind. Can't see anything because of the blood, and I don't have any suction." He laughed. "This'll be fun."

The deranged man cackled some more as he pushed the endotracheal tube into Dr. Graves' throat.

No, that isn't right! Dr. Graves yelled inside his head as the tube slipped into his esophagus instead of his trachea.

Carter removed the scope and attached a self-inflating bag to the end of the ET tube. He squeezed the bag, pushing air into Dr. Graves' stomach. "Dang." He patted the doctor's shoulder and said, "Hang in there, I'll give it another try." He pulled the tube out.

The laryngoscope scratched Dr. Graves' throat, and the killer cranked on it much harder this time, rocking it back against the doctor's front teeth. This time he shoved a cloth down into Dean's throat to soak up the blood before reattempting the intubation.

Oxygen starvation set Dr. Graves' world to spinning. Dark spots danced in his vision, and for a fleeting moment he thought, hoped, this would be what killed him. Then the ET tube slid into his trachea. The killer attached the bag again and inflated the doctor's lungs with air. "Second time's a charm." He hummed as he stood at the doctor's head, taping the tube in place and then compressing the bag every few seconds.

"Okay," he said after a couple of minutes, "that should be enough to hold you for a few minutes while I get started." He left the bag resting down on the doctor's upper chest.

Dr. Graves lay helpless, unable to move even an eyelid. He felt the killer attach another syringe to the IV tubing.

"I was hoping to score some roc—it lasts longer, you know. But all the ambulance had was succs, so I'll have to re-dose you every six or seven minutes or so. And I'll have to rush my cut-work." He laughed. "That's what I call my cutting artwork—cut-work." He sighed. "Maybe I'll have better luck finding some roc later today...for our second session."

No. Please, God, help me, Dr. Graves prayed.

"I think I'll start with the ribs," the killer said as he pumped another bagful of air into the doctor's lungs. "I'm sure I broke one or two last night; that should make it fairly easy to pry a couple up. I'll just cut right along the bruise, there."

No! Please help me! Dr. Graves prayed again.

Carter held a scalpel in his gloved hand and grinned down at his victim. "Now, this is going to hurt you much more than it does me." He laughed, then moved to Dr. Graves' side and slid the scalpel expertly through the skin between two ribs.

THIRTY FOUR

"I don't want to puncture your lung or sever an artery or anything, so I'm going to carefully dissect the tissue here so I can safely get to your ribs," the killer explained as his scalpel sliced through the muscle between two of Dr. Graves' ribs.

Exquisite sharp burning pain tore into him. It roused him through the haze of oxygen deprivation. Coherent thought became impossible, explosions of curse words and hatred for this maniac all that was left.

Carter set the scalpel on Dr. Graves' abdomen while he pumped the bag again, filling the doctor's lungs with air and his chest with agony. Then, the sizzle of burning flesh hit him as the killer cauterized the incision with a disposable Bovie.

Scalpel once more in hand, Carter made the final slice through the muscle before setting it down again. He slid his finger between the bone and tissue of the rib above the incision.

Dr. Graves screamed silently and ceaselessly, flooding his brain with misfiring synapses and electrical jolts.

Carter stretched the skin, tissue, and muscle away from the rib with one hand and closed his fingers around it with the other. He pulled, exerting steady, increasing pressure toward himself.

He stopped, head jerking up and toward the entrance to the cell. The doctor only registering that the pressure had let up.

Carter ran out the door, muttering, "What was that?"

A dull *thump* and quiet footsteps. Then Kat stood beside his head. He must be dreaming. Or dead, finally. But death shouldn't be full of agony. Death should end it.

"Oh, Dean." Kat pumped the bag as tears streamed down her face.

Where were the others? Did she bring the police? The screaming had stopped. Inside his head. *He'd* stopped screaming. He thought he'd been scared before. Scared of pain. Scared of dying. But he'd never known fear like now, this moment. Fear for Kat.

Kat removed her sweater and pressed it to the open wound before she moved to his other side to clamp the IV fluid and then wrestle open the restraint on his wrist. She glanced at the door then reached for the bag again. An angry grunt from the hallway got her attention. She grabbed one of the full syringes laying on the table and turned to face the threat.

The killer barreled into her, knocking her to the floor. Dr. Graves turned his head to see what was happening. He *turned his head.*

The succs was wearing off!

He trembled, and had no control over any other body part.

Kat slammed the needle into the killer's upper arm and depressed the plunger. Carter grabbed her hand and threw the syringe across the room. He wrapped one arm around her shoulders and pulled her back against his chest where they sat on the floor. He held a scalpel to her throat with the other hand, shaking like he'd fallen in an iced-over lake.

"I will kill you!" he seethed.

"Wait!" she said. "Wait. I just injected you with what I'm guessing is a neuromuscular blocker. I'm your only hope of surviving now."

"Dammit!" He tightened his grip around her. "You won't save me. Why would you save me? I'm nothing but a little bastard. My own dad wouldn't save me." His voice quieted to a near whisper. "You won't save me."

"I will." How was her voice so steady?

"You won't. So I'll kill you now, then the doctor. I won't be alone in death." His hold on her loosened, and his grip on the scalpel faltered, yet he still hung on.

"The police and ambulance are on their way. I'll breathe for you until they get here. I promise. I'm not a killer like you," she said.

"It shouldn't...take effect this fast... I'm—" He dropped the scalpel and his arm slipped from around her.

"I imagine adrenaline has something to do with that," she said, pushing his arm the rest of the way off herself. She jumped up and rushed to pump the bag for Dean. "I'm sorry. Please be okay. Please be okay." She stared into his eyes, the steadiness in her voice from a moment before, now metamorphosed into tremulous worry.

"You...promised." Carter collapsed the rest of the way to the floor.

Her eyes never leaving those of the doctor, she answered, "That I did. You'll be fine for a couple of minutes."

The trembling in Dr. Graves' limbs had decreased. He wiggled his fingers. He tried to draw in a breath on his own but the tube and bag were in the way. He raised his hand and touched Kat's arm.

Her eyes widened. "You can move!" She removed the tape holding the tube in place and gently pulled it out. "Can you breathe? Please be able to breathe."

He drew in a breath, squeezing his eyes shut against the pain.

"Okay. Good. Good." She glanced at the motionless killer behind her, then knelt beside the duffel bag, shuffling through the remaining contents. When she stood again, she held a flexible mask, the kind that would attach to the self-inflating bag. She attached them and knelt next to the killer. She rolled him all the way onto his back with some effort, tilted his head back, then placed the mask over his mouth and nose and watched his chest rise as she pumped air into him. She did this three times before returning to Dean's side.

"Kat," he said, his voice weak and raspy.

She brushed his hair back off his forehead and bit her trembling lip. "Dean, I'm so sorry...so sorry it took me so long."

He put his hand on her arm. "Don't. Apologize." He shook his head, too exhausted to continue. His body quaked and his teeth chattered together.

"Hang in there, Dean. The ambulance should be here soon." She undid the other restraints before breathing for the killer again. And, as if just realizing Dean was naked, she looked around almost frantically, her eyes falling to her sweater still pressed against his open chest wound. She grabbed the duffle bag and shook the contents out onto the floor, exclaiming "Yes!" when she saw what she needed. She ripped the package of the shiny emergency blanket with her teeth and unfolded it, growling with frustration when it didn't prove easy. Finally having accomplished the unfolding, she spread the thin, metallic blanket over his body, her eyes skipping over his genital region.

Dr. Graves found that having Kat see him naked and bleeding wasn't as embarrassing as he'd thought earlier. Intense agony and escaping a sure death had a way of making one not care about such things.

Kat looked at her phone and muttered, "Where are they? I called them twenty minutes ago."

She went back to the killer and breathed for him again, then paced beside Dean. The shivers had decreased and he tested out his ability to move beneath the blanket, wincing and grunting with each blessed movement of his limbs and painful breath pulled into his lungs of his own volition.

Sweat beaded on Dean's face. "How long has it been? Since you paralyzed him?"

Kat glanced back at the killer then down at her phone. "I'm not sure. It should last longer because I gave it in his muscle, right?"

"Yes. But..." He closed his eyes against the pain, speaking through clenched teeth, "Maybe again. To be safe."

She nodded and searched for another syringe. They'd fallen to the ground during the scuffle. She crawled around, looking under the table, her back to Carter.

"Looking for this?"

Kat turned to face the killer. He held a full syringe in his hand, barely a tremble to be seen. He sat up and lunged for her faster than should have been possible. She fell back, and he was on her quicker than she could scream. She grabbed his arm and pushed with both hands to keep the syringe away from her. The killer was still weakened from the medication, but he pressed down on her arms using his substantial weight. She wouldn't be able to keep it up much longer.

Dr. Graves growled in agony as he rolled off the table, clutching a scalpel in his unbroken hand. With a guttural cry, he pitched himself toward them and sank the scalpel into the side of the killer's neck, ripping it across the arteries and large veins there.

The killer jerked up, grabbed his neck, and fell to the side of Kat. She scrambled away from him as blood spurted through his fingers.

Dr. Graves rolled to his back, his vision darkened around the edges, and then all went blissfully dark.

THIRTY FIVE

Present Day
Dr. Graves

The killer, *maniacal grin pasted on his ashen face, advanced toward the lifeless Kat with a large scalpel, light from the flashlight glinting off its steel. Dr. Graves begged his body to move, but his muscles just weren't getting the crucial message. He tried to scream a warning at her, but it only sounded in his head.*

The killer bent over her, thrusting the scalpel toward her face—

Dr. Graves cried out with a jerk of pain. He opened his eyes, clammy sweat covering his body, as he looked around frantically, confused.

"Dean, it's okay. You're safe now."

As soon as his gaze met Kat's, he relaxed back into the pillow. He closed his eyes again and took some slow breaths, realizing that, though the pain was there, it was muted and tolerable. He opened his eyes, recognizing the muted walls and harsh lights of a hospital room. He turned his head to Kat again. "The killer?" His voice was barely a whisper, but she understood what he was asking.

"He's dead." She wiped the perspiration from his face with a cool cloth. "You killed him."

Memories of the torment surfaced and tears leaked from his eyes. Kat wiped those away, too, without a word. Then she sat in a chair right next to the bed and held his hand in silence.

He clung to her like a life raft while he tried to regain control of his emotions. He must have been on pain medication, that was the only explanation for not being able to master his reaction. Of course, he'd been through an extremely traumatic experience, but still. He should be able to control this. He turned his head away from Kat as he clamped down on his tremulous lips, the explosion of tears increasing.

Kat stood and laid her head gently on his chest, caressing his cheek with her hand. She didn't *shush* him or say a word. She just comforted him with her presence and her touch in a way he'd never felt before. So, he gave in and let himself cry for several minutes. When his tears were spent, he was shocked to find that he was stroking her head, his fingers finding solace in the softness of her hair.

"I'm sorry, Kat. You must be furious with me," he whispered.

She sat up, wiping tears from her own face without any shame. "Oh, I am." She smiled. "But we can discuss that later."

"How long was I out? What day is it?"

"It's early Monday. You started to wake up when we got here yesterday, but the doctors decided to keep you sedated. You had surgery to close the wound on your chest, and while you were out for that, they set the bones in your arm and leg and splinted them." She glanced at his nose. "You're going to have to have surgery on your nose sometime this week."

"Mmf," he grunted, too spent to say more, and he let his eyes drift closed.

"They have you on a morphine drip for the pain, and a couple of different antibiotics. That abandoned jail wasn't exactly as sterile as an operating room. You were already showing signs of infection."

He wanted to ask just one more question before the morphine and fatigue overtook him. He slurred, eyes still closed, "How long…"

"Shh." Kat resumed wiping his forehead with the cool cloth. "We'll talk later. Rest."

LIGHT STREAMED through the open blinds, and Dr. Graves squinted at the phlebotomist who'd awakened him when placing the tourniquet on his arm.

"Good afternoon, Dean." Kat's voice instantly soothed his pounding heart. He'd almost whacked the kid—the phlebotomist—with his splinted arm in an overzealous, startled reaction. Kat looked up at the young man and said, kindly, "Next time, you should wake him up by talking to him first." She smiled. "That way you won't startle him."

The young man—Trevor, according to his badge—nodded with a shy smile. "Good idea. I'll do that."

Dr. Graves' mouth felt like he'd been crawling through the desert for days with nothing to drink. After the phlebotomist finished up and left the room, he asked, "Is there any water in here?" His voice came out all gruff and raspy.

"Yes. They said you could have some sips of water and see how you do before giving you anything else." Kat held a large hospital mug up. "Do you want to try sitting up a little?"

He nodded. Yeah, sitting up would be good after laying flat for…a long time.

She pushed the button to raise the head of the bed. "Tell me when."

"That's good," he said, trying not to wince at the tug in his ribs. Then, before he could even try to figure out how to do it himself, Kat held the mug close to him and maneuvered the straw into his mouth. He took several big sips and would have taken more, but Kat pulled it away.

"Take it easy," she said. "Let's make sure that stays down before you get carried away."

He rested his head back against the pillow, hating how it felt to be near helpless. When Kat turned back around from setting the water on the bedside table, he got a good look at her. Little strands of her hair had come loose from her ponytail, she had circles under her eyes, and there were splotches of dust and blood on her clothes. Dr. Graves narrowed his eyes. "How long have you been here? Have you even been home?"

Kat looked down at her clothes and then tried to smooth the stray hairs on her head. "I've been here since they brought you in. I wanted to make sure you weren't alone when you woke up." She lowered her eyes. "I know you don't have anyone else since your mom died last year."

Something clogged in his throat. He swallowed. "You..." He coughed and swallowed a couple more times, then tried again. "You didn't have to do that."

"I wanted to." Kat sounded like she had something stuck in her throat, too. She looked away, wiping at her cheek. "If I'd only talked you out of it, or got there sooner, or insisted that the police come with me..." Her voice broke.

"Kat." He took her hand and squeezed, willing her to look at him. "This isn't your fault. The fact is that you *saved* me." He cleared his throat again and just let the tears slide down his face. He wasn't about to let go of her warm hand to wipe at them. "If you hadn't shown up"—he shook his head—"I'd be dead. Or worse, I'd still be alive. He'd still be torturing me. Cutting me up like his own living cadaver."

Kat snorted and finally looked at him, her wearied smile softening the haggard look. "Cadavers aren't alive, Dean."

He wasn't quite ready to smile yet, but he gave her his best eye-roll. "You know what I meant." He looked over at the chair next to his bed. A disposable pillow sat atop a folded-up blanket. "Have you gotten any sleep the last two days?"

She shrugged. "A little."

He gave her his sternest I'm-the-boss look. "Go home and get some sleep. I'll be fine."

"Yeah," Detective Fitzpatrick said as he walked into the room, "and take a shower. You stink."

"Pup!" Kat smiled. "What a nice thing to say."

The detective winked, a smile touching his lips. "I'm a nice guy, what can I say?" The glint in his eyes faded and all playfulness dropped from his face. "But, seriously, Kat, go home. Davis is just outside the room; he'll give you a ride so you don't fall asleep at the wheel. I'll stay with the good doctor until you get back."

Kat hesitated, looking from Pup to Dr. Graves, working at her bottom lip with her teeth.

"Go home, Katherine," Dr. Graves said sternly. He moved his gaze to the detective. "And I don't need a babysitter, Detective Fitzpatrick." He looked down at his hands, his voice a notch quieter as he added, "But I appreciate the offer...and maybe you can stay for a little while and answer some questions I have."

"Sure, doc, I'd be happy to."

"*Doctor*—" He shook his head. "Screw it. Go ahead and call me 'doc'."

"Ah, man! That takes all the fun out of it!" Fitzpatrick teased.

Kat leaned over Dr. Graves, her cheek brushed his as she put her lips next to his ear, and his breath caught. She whispered, "I won't be gone long. I'm here for you. We'll get through this together."

With an impulse that shocked him to his core, he cradled her head in his hand, pressing her face against his. The warmth from her skin touching his like a fire. He squeezed his eyes shut and just allowed himself this moment of intense comfort, for once not analyzing the unusual sensations he only encountered around Kat.

Fitzpatrick cleared his throat, breaking the spell. *Jerk.*

With a sigh, Dr. Graves put his hand back down at his side. Kat stood and stared into his eyes for a few beats of his heart. Afraid to speak, he nodded, not breaking eye contact. She squeezed his arm and nodded back before turning to leave. She paused at the door and looked back at the detective. "I won't be long. Thank you, Troy."

"You bet," he said. He strolled over to the bedside chair and lowered himself into it with a grunt.

Dr. Graves closed his eyes and took a breath. "I suppose you'll be wanting to question me."

"Whenever you're ready, doc. That's not why I'm here."

He didn't know how much more of nice-agreeable-Detective-Fitzpatrick he could take. He closed his eyes and steeled himself with a deep breath that tore at the stitches in his chest. "Let's get it over with."

THIRTY SIX

Present Day
Dr. Graves

Sitting up in a chair, free from IV tubing and monitor wires, Dr. Graves turned the TV on out of sheer boredom—and maybe a touch of nervousness. Detective Davis had swapped places with Detective Fitzpatrick sometime during the night and had been snoring loudly in the recliner when the nurse had come in to take his vital signs. The detective turned a slight shade of pink and mumbled something about coffee when the nurse mentioned "bed bath."

As nice as it had been to sponge off, Dr. Graves couldn't wait until they'd let him take an actual shower, he could still smell stale vomit even though his hair had been scrubbed a couple of times. "Tomorrow," the nurse had said. For now, he was just grateful to be out of that bed. He flipped through channels, not really paying attention to what was on. Kat had called to let him know she was on her way, apologizing profusely for not coming back sooner, for sleeping far longer than she'd planned. "You needed the sleep," he'd assured her. "And I was sleeping, too, most of that time. No need to apologize."

His thumb froze on the remote as his own face filled the TV screen. It was the picture the state of Georgia used for his I.D. badge. He turned up the volume.

"...Graves and Katherine Flanagan stopped the killer we've dubbed The Doctor of Death from his reign of terror. The police have released the killer's name, Carter Ridge, an Anesthesiologist who worked at various surgical centers around the city."

Dr. Graves hit the off button with disgust. "He wasn't a doctor," he said to the TV.

Kat stepped through the door and looked around the small room. "Who were you talking to?"

His irritation at the incompetence of journalists these days dissipated somewhat at the sight of Kat looking refreshed and holding two tall cups of coffee in her hands. "Oh, well, the TV I guess. Did you hear what they're calling him? The killer?"

She glanced at the blank screen and raised an eyebrow as she handed him one of the steaming cups. "I've heard a couple of different monikers they're using. Which are you referring to that has you so up in arms?"

Before answering, he took a sip of the coffee, savoring the burn to his tongue and throat. "Doctor," he said. "They're calling him a doctor."

Kat pulled a plastic chair over next to him and sat. "Well, the distinction between anesthesiologists and nurse anesthetists can be confusing for lay people."

"Journalists aren't lay people. Or at least they shouldn't be. It's their job to get things right and know the difference."

With a roll of her eyes and a charming twist to her mouth, Kat shook her head. "It's been a while since journalism had the integrity and drive to 'get things right' that you're still trying to attribute to them. Is this the first story you've seen on...on the murders?" She was right.

"Yes, it is. Now I remember why I don't watch the news anymore. You said they have other names for...for Carter. What else are they calling him?"

"The main one is The Bar Killer, since he picked up all his victims from bars."

"Well, that's at least accurate," Dr. Graves said.

Kat gave him an appraising look. "You look better. How does it feel to be sitting up, out of bed?"

"Better. But I really just want to get out of here and back to my own house." He didn't know how he was going to take care of himself with two fractured limbs and various other major bodily injuries. He might have to hire a nurse. The thought of a stranger in his home made him scowl.

As if she'd read his mind, Kat said, "Well, when they decide to cut you loose, I'm coming home with you. There's no way you can care for yourself in this shape."

"Kat—"

Her warm finger on his lips did more than quiet him. His heart stuttered and then restarted at a much higher rate than normal.

"Dr. Graves," she said, "this isn't open to discussion. I'm going to stay with you until I'm certain you're well enough to take care of yourself. The end."

Well, how could he argue with that? For possibly the first time in his life, he swallowed his pride—and the lump in his throat was almost enough to choke on. He nodded then looked down at his hands, his voice barely a whisper, and said, "Thank you, Kat."

"You're welcome." She touched his arm and waited for him to look at her. "And thank you for not arguing with me about it." A small, victorious smirk touched her lips.

Kat's timing turned out to be impeccable, as usual. As they sat in comfortable silence, sipping their coffee, the nurse entered. She took his vital signs and checked his bandages. "Good news. You've been cleared to have the nasal surgery in the morning. The ENT, Dr. Kelly, will be in later today to go over the procedure with you and get the consent signed."

Dr. Graves huffed. "That's good news?"

The nurse laughed. "Well, it is if you want to get released. They plan on surgery tomorrow and home the next day as long as all goes well and we can set up some help for you."

Kat leaned forward. "That's all taken care of." Pink flushed her cheeks as she continued. "I'll be staying with Dr. Graves while he recovers."

With a slight raise of an eyebrow, the nurse said, "Fantastic. That makes the discharge planning so much easier." She paused, shaking her head. "And it will calm the fight between the young, single nurses who've all volunteered to apply for a spot to be your home nurse."

Kat laughed. "Even with a broken nose and black and blue coloring your face the girls can't stay away."

"Well..." Heat rose up his neck. "I...I don't...uh..."

The nurse and Kat both laughed at his discomfort. Kat patted his arm. "It's okay, Dean. I'll see if we can put your 'Augusta's Most Eligible Bachelor' status on hold. At least until you're back on your feet."

He scowled and suddenly found the plastic lid of his coffee cup to be profoundly interesting.

—∿—

Dr. Graves studied himself in the bathroom mirror the morning after his nasal surgery. He turned his head back and forth, inspecting the external splint that looked a little ridiculous but wasn't uncomfortable. The worst part, though, was not being able to breathe through his nose at all. He took a slow, deep breath in through his mouth then pursed his lips as he forcefully released it, trying to calm the unsettled feeling in his chest. The surgeon offered to send him home with a Xanax prescription to help with the anxiety caused by the nasal packing, but he declined. He could deal with it for five days.

Sitting in a wheelchair, wearing borrowed scrubs, he waited in the hospital room while Kat picked up his prescriptions at the hospital pharmacy. He tapped his fingers on the armrest and concentrated on taking more slow, deep breaths through his mouth. He was going to need some lip balm; he licked his lips, even while knowing it would only dry them out more.

After what seemed like hours, Kat returned, carrying a small white paper bag and followed by one of the nurses. She dug in the bag and came out with a small tube of lip balm. "Here." She handed it to him. "I figured you might need this. I'm going to take your stuff out to the car and pull up to the patient loading doors." Kat smiled at the nurse. "Ashley will wheel you out."

He almost asked her if she could read his mind, but just thanked her instead before slathering his dry lips with petroleum-based goo. His "stuff" consisted of a plastic "patient belongings" bag packed with hospital toiletries like a toothbrush and toothpaste, his water mug, a comb, etc. The remnants of his clothing had been bagged up at the scene and logged into the evidence locker down at the police station.

Ashley did one last set of vital signs and removed the IV catheter from his arm before wheeling him out to Kat's car. It took both Kat and the nurse to help him transfer from the wheelchair into the car. His knees threatened to give and tumble them all to the ground, but he clenched his jaw and found the strength to stand on one leg long enough to turn and plop unceremoniously—and somewhat painfully —into the passenger seat. He'd become surprisingly weak in just a few days. Getting his strength back was priority number one.

They stopped at a medical supply store to get a knee scooter and a drive-thru to get lunch. By the time they reached his house, he used the knee scooter to get to the porch, sat on his butt to struggle up the stairs backwards while Kat carried the scooter up, and finally got settled in his recliner—his number one priority had changed to taking a nap.

THIRTY SEVEN

Kat and Dr. Graves fell into a busy routine over the next few days. He was pleased to find that Kat was a great cook, and surprised to discover how much he enjoyed her company. He'd eaten dinners alone for so many years, he'd been worried that having her there would be irritating and he wouldn't be able to hide that from her. But it turned out to be completely the opposite. Their conversations were fun and intelligent. And the rare moments of silence weren't weird. Kat, unlike most people he'd been around, didn't find it necessary to fill every moment with speaking, she was just as comfortable eating in silence as he was. But it didn't often come to that.

He realized early on that Kat was *interesting*, and he looked forward to hearing her take on things even if it differed vastly from his own opinions. Maybe even especially then.

And she didn't for one moment let him wallow in self-pity. She was great to help him when necessary, but insisted he try to do things for himself first. And he insisted on doing all the *personal* things by himself, even if it took him four times longer than normal.

Dr. Graves refused to take anything stronger than ibuprofen after a couple of days on pain medication. It took him hours to fall asleep the first night without the sedating effect of a narcotic. The necessity of breathing through his mouth didn't help that endeavor. He finally drifted off, and fell right into panic.

He couldn't see the killer's face but watched, helpless, as he injected something directly into the doctor's neck like they always do in unrealistic TV shows. The next breath he tried to draw in ended at his closed throat. His chest heaved, but no air reached his lungs. It didn't even reach his trachea. It danced around his lips, teasing him but never entering where it was so desperately needed.

Flailing his arms, the thought that he shouldn't be able to move at all flitted across his brain. The medication. The killer. Paralysis. He roared, releasing his last held breath, and flipped to his side, dodging an unseen terror.

With a *thud*, he slammed into the floor, pain reverberating through his body like bass at a rock concert. His ribs, his arm and leg, the incision site, his head, and his nosc all screamed at him. Realization that it had just been a dream, a nightmare, hit. He closed his eyes and concentrated on breathing through his mouth, afraid to move, a few tears leaking from the outer corners of his eyes.

Kat crashed through the door and flipped on the light. Dr. Graves' whole body jerked and his eyes flew open, the adrenaline from the dream and the fall still running rampant through his veins. He tried to hold in the moan ramping up in his throat, but managed only to turn it into a higher pitch as it escaped through his vocal cords.

Kat gasped. Then she was at his side, on her knees. "What happened? I'm so sorry! Are you okay?"

Closing his eyes again, he said, "Give me...just...a minute."

Warm fingers found his hand and held it in silence while he gathered himself both physically and emotionally. He clenched his jaw, then panicked a little when he realized he couldn't breathe. He squeezed Kat's hand hard, but she didn't pull away, and opened his mouth for a ragged breath.

The pain eased up and he looked up at Kat, worry creasing her face. "I had a nightmare. Then fell out of bed." He tried to smile but his lips didn't quite make the trip. "Like a child."

"You lived through a real nightmare; I'm not surprised your mind is revisiting it in your sleep." She gently brushed his hair back from his clammy forehead and whispered, "My mind keeps revisiting it while I'm awake."

He didn't want to talk about this. "Will you help me get untangled from these sheets and check my incision, please? I fear I may have ripped a stitch or two."

"Yes, of course." She pushed her hair behind her ears before gently tugging the sheets away from him. She lifted his t-shirt and winced. "You're bleeding through the dressing. I'll need to take it off and clean the blood up before I can see if you've pulled any stitches out."

She disappeared into the master bathroom for a moment and returned with a warm, wet washcloth. He watched her face, telling himself it was rude to stare but staring anyway. The tenderness in her touch and the concern in her eyes affected him in a way he'd never felt before. A surge of emotion welled up inside him and he had to fight not to sob out loud. Forced to look away from her, he turned his head to the side, tightening his hands into fists. His breath hitched, and he couldn't stop the small sound from escaping.

"Am I hurting you?" Kat paused in her ministrations.

Dr. Graves shook his head, still turned away from her.

"Look at me," she demanded softly.

He pinched his eyes shut and drew in a breath before slowly turning to look at her. Her messy hair, Aerosmith t-shirt, plaid pajama pants, bare feet, then back to her eyes.

And the damned *feelings* attacked his throat again.

"Talk to me, Dean. What's going on in that brilliant head of yours?"

"Too many things." He cringed when his voice quavered.

Kat nodded, looking into his eyes a moment longer before returning to her task, gently wiping the wound now that the dressing was off. "When you're ready," she said, "I'll be here to listen."

Relief flooded him, and he relaxed his hands. He would need to sort through his thoughts and feelings before trying to talk about them. More than sort through, he needed to do a deep dive.

"It looks like the sutures are all intact, a couple of them just got tugged a little and the incision opened up between them. Do you think we should call the surgeon?"

"No." The last thing Dean wanted to do was go back to the hospital. "It'll be fine."

"Okay," Kat said. "But I'm calling in the morning."

She covered the wound with clean dressings then helped him back into bed. She laid the covers over him and, without a word of explanation, retrieved her pillow and blanket from the spare room and lay down beside him. He pulled his arm out from under the blanket and entwined his fingers with hers, laying their hands on the bed between them.

⎯⋀⎯

SEVERAL HOURS LATER, Dr. Graves awoke in the same position, his hand still curled around Kat's. In the light of early morning, his reaction—both to the dream and to Kat—seemed overblown. Yet, he was reluctant to release his grip. His heart fluttered at the thought of it. But his bladder didn't care about his heart. He started to ease his hand away from hers, trying not to wake her, and her fingers tightened around his.

"Dean?" Her sleepy voice made him smile. "You okay?"

"As good as can be expected, but nature calls."

"Oh!" She released his hand. "Let me help you up." She rolled off the bed, retrieved his scooter, and pushed it next to him.

His first attempt to roll to his side sent shards of pain slicing through his body. He held his breath and tried again, this time succeeding. Kat offered her hand and steeled herself as he used it to pull up to a sitting position. He glared at the scooter, surprising himself both by the hatred he felt for an inanimate object and the sudden desire to have the wheelchair from the hospital back. But again, his bladder didn't care.

He again held his breath as he heaved himself off the bed, balancing on one foot, and settled his knee onto the scooter. He let go of Kat and gripped the handlebar with his good hand. Progress was slow, but he eventually made it the five feet from his bed to the bathroom.

"I'll be right out here if you need me," Kat called.

His face flushed as he considered that she could hear him urinating. He rolled his eyes at himself; that was the least of his worries. He could hear Kat busying herself around his bedroom while he did his business. *One more day until this packing is out of my nose and the splints on my arm and leg are replaced with casts. Then I'll be able to take care of myself.* Somehow, that thought didn't comfort him as the memory of Kat's hand in his, her quiet support, her caring eyes —all flooded his mind.

THIRTY EIGHT

Present Day
Dr. Graves

Nasal packing removed, new Ravenclaw-colored casts on his arm and leg, bruises healing to a dull brown, and his incision closing up nicely—Dr. Graves was ready to be on his own. *Kat needs to get back to work,* he told himself. The morgue was probably a disaster without at least one of them there. The city had brought a per diem medical examiner in to take his place while he was recovering, and the thought of someone else messing up his instruments and getting crumbs in his keyboard and joking around with Detectives Fitzpatrick and Davis...well, he just needed to get back to work, too.

So, a week after leaving the hospital, he found himself alone for the first time since the...incident. He scooted out onto his back porch, a water-bottle full of cream soda resting in the basket on the handlebars, and settled into his chair. He leaned his head back and closed his eyes, his thoughts, as they so often did these days, floating to Kat.

A cold, wet nose nuzzled his hand. His joy at seeing Winston there, tennis ball at his feet, shocked him a little. He knew deep down that he enjoyed the dog's company, but he'd never admit that out loud.

Maybe he should consider getting a dog of his own. A bit of companionship sounded nice, along with an early warning system in the form of barking should any strangers approach his house. Something he'd never worried about before...

"Sorry, Winston." He scratched the dog's ears. "I'm not in good enough shape to play fetch with you today." As if he completely understood, Winston sat, resting his head on Dr. Graves' lap. Leaning his head back, Dr. Graves closed his eyes and continued to run his fingers through the dog's fur. The gentle breeze and sunshine soothed his aching soul. His thoughts again turned to Kat.

Maybe he should call and see how her first day back was going?

He awkwardly dug his phone out of his pocket and clicked it to life. Among the twenty or so missed calls, Kat's name stood out. She'd called just a few minutes ago, just after The Augusta Chronicle and just before CNN. He shook his head; the reporters were why he'd turned his phone to silent to begin with. He was not going to grant *any* interviews. They could get their information from the police report.

He clicked on Kat's name and hit the *call* icon.

She answered on the second ring. "Hey, Dr. Graves, I was just getting ready to call again. How are you doing? Do you need anything?"

Her voice was like puppet strings attached to the corners of his mouth, pulling it up into a too-big smile. He swallowed, the skin of his neck and face heating up. "I'm okay," he said. "Just hanging out on the patio with the neighbor's dog." He snickered a little at the adoration in the dog's eyes staring up at him.

"What?" Kat asked.

"Nothing. I'm just finally realizing what people see in dogs. How is your day going? Are things a mess there?"

"Well, I've definitely got a lot of catching up to do, but I'll have everything back in order by the time you come back."

"What would I do without you." He winced as the words left his mouth in a much more serious tone than he'd planned.

Kat to the rescue with her lighthearted reply, "Probably drown in a pile of paperwork if this office is any indication of what goes on here without me."

His chuckle was followed by an awkward silence. Why was it always awkward when the conversation was taking place via phone call? He cleared his throat and rushed to fill the void. "I was thinking that for dinner tonight I'd try out that delivery app you made me download. Mexican food from Casa del Rey, if you'd like to join me." He closed his eyes and rushed to say, "That is...if you haven't had your fill of me. I understand if you need a break."

The teasing note to her voice made the tightness in his throat relax. "Well...you are a lot to handle. But Casa is my favorite, so I'll fight through the annoyance in exchange for delicious chips and salsa."

"Yes, good chips and salsa could bring world peace. I'll schedule the delivery for seven, but feel free to come earlier if you'd like."

"I'll head over after work. Do you need me to bring anything?"

Just your smile. He rolled his eyes at himself. "Nope. Unless you want something to drink besides water or cream soda."

"Okay. See you then."

─∿─

ANOTHER WEEK PASSED, AND DR. GRAVES' bruises were mostly faded. He'd worked hard each day to build up his stamina, wincing at the thought of his left calf and arm muscles atrophying away beneath the casts. He fought with both Human Resources and his primary care doctor about returning to work—neither of them felt he was ready. But in the end, he wore them down, and here he stood on the front porch with his left leg resting on the cushion of the scooter he'd come to despise. Kat had insisted on driving him. He straightened up as her car turned into his drive. She'd checked in on him almost every day in person and several times a day by phone, and he found himself missing her whenever she wasn't there. He'd had a lot of time to think about his feelings—too much time—and yet he was just as confused about them now as he had been at the first tingle.

He pushed off and wheeled down the gently angled, temporary ramp his neighbor—Winston's human—had built for him after seeing him scoot down the stairs on his behind. He'd come over and quietly installed it without saying a word. The only reason Dr. Graves' knew who'd done it was because he caught a glimpse of him as he headed back across his yard, toolbox in tow.

Good people. There were still so many good people in this world.

Kat stepped out of her car and smiled as she walked around to open the passenger door for him. Once inside the car with his seatbelt buckled, Kat handed him a cup of coffee. Their fingers brushed during the hand-off, and he lingered before taking hold of the cup, prolonging the contact. The memory of holding her hand all night after having a nightmare floated into his head, and he couldn't tear his eyes away from hers for a few seconds. He cleared his throat, took the coffee, and diverted his gaze to the windshield. Confusion flooded his mind again.

"Are you ready for this?" Kat asked as she backed into the street.

"I was ready a week ago," he grumbled.

Kat laughed, shaking her head.

His phone buzzed. He fished it out of his pocket and whispered, "And it begins," before answering on speaker so Kat could hear. "Dr. Graves."

"Hey, Graves!" Fitzpatrick's voice blared.

"*Doctor* Graves." Old habits die hard.

"Yeah, that's what I meant, doc."

Dr. Graves sighed. "What do you want, detective?"

"We have a welcome back case for you. We're bagging him up now so he should be at the morgue within the hour."

His stomach twisted. He turned his head so Kat couldn't see the blood drain from his face. *Please don't be a murder.* "Well, are you going to tell me about it, or did you just call to annoy me?" His voice sounded a bit gruff, but at least it didn't get caught on the sudden contractures in his throat on its way out.

"I was gettin' to it, sheesh. I thought you'd be in a better mood on your first day back."

Dr. Graves could hear the smile in the detective's voice, and some of the tension left his shoulders. He wouldn't be joking around if it was a murder. "I haven't finished my coffee yet."

"That explains it. The deceased is a twenty-three-year-old male, found unresponsive by his roommate after the roommate heard him fall. An ambulance was called, but resuscitation attempts failed. Apparently the deceased had been playing a computer game for over twenty hours, hadn't had anything to eat or drink that the roommate knew of, and—get this—hadn't even bothered to leave his chair to relieve himself. It reeks of urine in here."

"Now that's dedication..." Kat mumbled.

"No," Dr. Graves said. "That's addiction."

"Yeah," Detective Fitzpatrick agreed. "I think I'll throw away my kids' video game console when I get home. Anyway, the roommate mentioned that he'd probably been live-streaming as he played, so our tech guy is looking to see if it was recorded. Might help you figure out what happened."

"Oh, I'm pretty sure I know what happened," he said as Kat pulled into the parking lot. "See you when you get here." He ended the call before the detective could respond.

A calmness he hadn't felt in weeks enveloped him as he scooted into the morgue. Kat had rearranged things just enough to make getting around with the knee scooter easier. The odor of chemicals and cleaning supplies filled his nose with a familiarity he hadn't known he'd been craving. He paused beside the metal exam table and inhaled deeply. Opening his eyes, he caught Kat staring at him with a smirk. He cleared his throat and grinned a little sheepishly. "I, uh, kind of missed it here."

"I can tell." She held open the door to the hallway that led to their offices. "After you, boss."

Sitting behind his desk gave him the same feeling of peace as the scents of the morgue had. He logged into his computer and started going through emails, most of which went directly to the trash bin—either outdated or garbage to begin with, like anything that looked remotely like it had come from a reporter.

The elevator *dinged*, signaling the body had arrived. Kat met him at his door where he balanced on one leg and clumsily pulled his lab coat on. He'd requested that the orthopedic doctor make the part of the cast encircling his thumb webbing to be as narrow as possible so he could still hold and use instruments. Still, he was thankful it was his left arm that had been injured and not his right.

As the EMTs lifted the bag onto the exam table, Dr. Graves said to Kat, "Get the x-ray machine ready, we'll be doing a chest view first thing."

The EMTs helped remove the body from the bag and turned their heads away at the strong odor of urine. "Whew!" one of them exclaimed. "We'll leave you to it, doctor. We need to get back in service. It's good to see you back at work."

Dr. Graves nodded. "Thanks for your help."

The EMTs hurried through the sliding doors then loaded their stretcher onto the elevator, waving as it closed.

Kat shot the chest x-ray and pulled it up on the screen. "What in the world?"

"What do you see?" Dr. Graves asked in his teacher's voice.

"His heart. It's...misshapen or something. Like it's almost twisted or backwards."

Nodding, he pointed at the silhouette of the heart. "See how the right side is bigger than the left ventricle? What do you think could cause that?"

He could see the wheels spinning in Kat's head as she narrowed her eyes at the screen. "The right side should be smaller than the left because it doesn't have to work as hard, just pumping blood to the lungs where the pressure is lower." She looked at him, eyebrows raised in question.

"Correct." He waited for her to continue.

"Pulmonary hypertension could cause it to enlarge, but he was young and it's unlikely he had a heart defect—there's no surgery scar on his chest. I guess he could have had an undiagnosed problem, but again, unlikely." She folded her arms and tilted her head to the side, crinkling her brows. Then she straightened up and looked at the doctor. "Something blocked the blood from flowing. A blood clot."

"Yes!" Dr. Graves squeezed her shoulder in his delight at her ability to retain knowledge. "Yes. This is a classic sign of an acute, massive pulmonary embolism."

"From being immobile for so many hours," Kat added.

He nodded. "Exactly. One or more blood clots formed in his legs over the twenty-plus hours he remained stationary, and when he stood up the clot broke free and went straight to his pulmonary artery, blocked the blood flow into the lungs, making the right ventricle blow up like a balloon, and eventually his heart stopped from lack of oxygen."

The autopsy was a comparatively short one. Once he opened the chest and sliced carefully into the heart, his theory was proven to be the case. He pulled out a large clot wedged in the pulmonary artery and extending along the length of the pulmonary artery tree. He also found blood clots in the arteries of both lower legs.

Kat closed up the incisions, slid the body into a locker, and cleaned up the morgue while Dr. Graves dictated the autopsy report. Kat agreed to stay late so he could get caught up on some things, and by the time exhaustion would allow him to do no more, it was twilight, the sun barely peeking over the horizon.

He insisted on opening the driver side door for Kat as they reached her car, but he paused, looking at the ground. His mind had been churning for the last hour—really, for the last two weeks. Longer if he was honest with himself. Maybe it was the fatigue plaguing him, or maybe his brain was overloaded and he needed to relieve some of the mental pressure, but he opened his mouth and words spilled out.

"I've been having some feelings I don't really understand. Maybe you can help me make some sense of them." He glanced up at her.

"Okay. I'm listening," she said softly, leaning her hip and shoulder against the car.

He gripped the scooter's handlebar tightly, his knuckles turning white. "First," he started. "I want to be in physical contact with you—which is weird because I've never much liked touching people or them touching me." He didn't dare look up to see her expression, he just hurried to continue. "I think about you, a lot, when you aren't near me...and when you *are* near me." His lips pulled up into a half-smile. "Thinking about you and being near you makes my heart rate increase...makes me warm...makes me queasy, but in a good way, you know?"

He dared a quick glance at her. Her expression was soft, her beautiful, dark eyes intense. He swallowed. "And when we touch, even just a brush of skin when you hand me something, this tangible, yet indescribable feeling shoots through me. In my thirty-four years of life, I've never felt any of these things before. I didn't believe such feelings existed. I rolled my eyes at such things." He paused again with a nervous chuckle.

Knowing on some instinctual level that he *had* to meet her gaze when he said this next part, he looked into her now glistening eyes. "What I'm trying to say, Kat, is I'm in love with you. I always thought love was a myth, something people made up. But now I know it's real."

Kat sucked in a breath and covered her mouth with a hand, her glistening eyes now full on pouring out the tears.

Dr. Graves licked his lips and shrugged. "I don't know what I should do now," he said awkwardly.

Kat stepped closer and gently touched his face, letting her hand fall to his chest. "You should kiss me."

And if he thought just touching her set off sparks—as their lips melded together, the tingling sparks turned into a full-on fireworks show blasting his nerve endings.

Hmm, he thought, *love really is real.*

EPILOGUE

D r. Graves smiled as he watched Kat's perfect cast. This time, on their second fishing trip together, their target was catfish. Hopefully giant ones.

She glanced over at him and returned his smile, hers just a bit smug. "You'd better get your line out there. Remember, this is a competition."

"And what's the prize?" He quirked an eyebrow.

"Bragging rights, of course." Kat returned his raised eyebrow with one of her own, but added an adorable smirk. "Unless you had... something else...in mind."

Still unaccustomed to her open flirtation in their recent change from strictly business to post-confession of his love to her, heat rose up his neck. "I...uh..." He had no idea what to say to that. His phone buzzed in his pocket and he turned his back to her to answer it as she laughed at his awkwardness.

"Dr. Graves," he answered.

"Dr. Graves, this is Dr. Michaels from the Georgia Department of Public Health. I could really use your expertise with a developing problem."

"What's the problem, and how can I help?"

"I'm afraid we're at the beginning stages of an epidemic. We've seen eight deaths in the last month of young, healthy individuals stricken with severe pneumonia. Currently, in the state of Georgia, we know of ten more who are hospitalized, six of those in ICU. This is on top of a rise in pneumonia hospitalizations and deaths in high-risk individuals." Dr. Michaels cleared his throat. "I know it's the weekend, but can you come to Atlanta, Dr. Graves? Today?"

ABOUT THE AUTHOR

 Holli Anderson has a Bachelor's Degree in Nursing—which has nothing to do with writing, except maybe by adding some pretty descriptive injury and vomit scenes to her books. She discovered her joy of writing during a very trying period in her life when escaping into make-believe saved her. She enjoys reading any book she gets her hands on.

Along with her husband, Steve, and their four sons, she lives in Grantsville, Utah—the same small town in which she grew up.

This has been an
Immortal Production